HOW I MADE IT OVER

HOW I MADE IT OVER

Victorious Life Stories

DR. TONYA BLACKMON

Conglomerate Empowerment

Reverend Mother Lorraine Barnes

Mother of Jacqueline "Lulu" Brown & Founder: Diamond in the Rough to Jewel of Treasure

Today we pay tribute and dedicate this book to Mother Barnes for all she has done. We honor her talents, unique qualities and give acknowledgment and recognition due to her efforts and hard work, however big or small. We recognize, honor, and thank her for being a bright light that has eliminated the darkness in our lives. We honor and cherish the light within ourselves that she helped put there and in the world around us.

At 93 years of age, she is currently an Elder at New Beginnings Outreach Ministry, under the pastoral leadership of Pastor Rosa Clemons. Mother Barnes is loving, forgiving, and concerned about her family, church, and community. Therefore, she has many spiritual children that can't be counted. She remains active in her praying, mentoring, and love for others.

Contents

I

You are Valuable- Your Story Matters

Dr. Tonya Blackmon

".. Man does not live on bread alone, but on every word that comes from the mouth of God." Matthew 4:4

I am Dr. Tonya Blackmon, and I am a domestic violence survivor. One of my earliest childhood memories was watching my stepdad physically abuse my mother. I have faint memories of childhood rape. I have survived abuse from those closest to me and in the military. One boyfriend slapped me the taste out of mouth. Every man that I have ever loved was unfaithful. Family and friends have said and done the craziest things against me. During and after therapy, I had to question why I accepted that type of treatment from others. Honestly, I do not know the answer. And today that is simply fine with me. Smile.

Here is what I have learned. We do not have to know all the answers to life's questions to be victorious. We just need to know that we are valuable and our stories matter. Because you are valuable, consider the following questions.

- What do you really want?
- What do you like/dislike?
- How do you want to be treated by loved ones and friends?
- What makes you smile?
- What makes you angry?
- And if you are business owner like me, do you enjoy serving clients or producing your products?

After you have answered those questions, begin to set boundaries TODAY. You are Valuable. On purpose, I encourage you to put your desires, needs, peace and happiness, and self-care first. Do not be like me. At the age of 40 years old, I decided that I was going to stop allowing people- my relatives, husband, children, anyone to misuse me. Because of this, I was slandered and called selfish, a few other choice words, but it did not matter to me. I am Free to live life on my own terms. You are too! I give you permission to say Enough is Enough. I can't hear you. Stream, "Enough is Enough!"

To me, each person is valuable and has a story to share. Here is a piece of my story...

As I have matured, I learned to be enormously proud to be from a rural town in the South, because nothing compares to being raised by a community of loved ones on a dirt road. Because I wanted out of the small-town environment as a teenager, I joined the military. While in the service I learned discipline, leadership, how to teach others and the trials of being in a war. I made a promise to myself that if I made it back home safe from the Persian Gulf, that I was going to complete my college education, raise a family and enjoy the good American life. My military career enabled me to interact with people from all around the world. As I travel for business, on purpose, I create situations where I connect with people from diverse cultures. My husband and I are humbled by our life experiences.

Before I go any further -- Let me tell you that the person you see today is vastly different from the person I was for most of my life. From 1993 to 2015, I was a dreamer. I was a people pleaser. I was a procrastinator. Although, I started my business in 2009, I kept my day job. And ultimately, I was fearful of leaving my corporate job and taking the leap into becoming a full-time business owner. Imagine -- for 12 years -- that was me! Now, there is absolutely nothing wrong with working a full-time job and running a side hustle business simultaneously. I strongly believe that each person needs to have at least 3-7 revenue generating streams.

Here is why I share this with you...

We are living in a global, modern day 1930s Great Depression era. Due to COVID-19, hundreds of thousands of people from around the world have lost their main source of income. Globally, the unemployment rates, business closures, and eviction notices have skyrocketed. Some children have still not gone back to school. At the time of this writing, one of my son's called and shared that his job is permanently closing. I do not want it to take a tragedy or something unfortunate in your life, to snap you into living your best life and wake up!

That is what it took for me.

On April 2015, my husband and I got a call that changed our lives. We were anticipating our second granddaughter's birth and excited. We had the baby shower, the name picked out, and the room decorated. We were ready for Cassidy Michelle's arrival. Then we got the call that something was not right. As we drove the 45-minute drive to the hospital, I had a hard time breathing. I was unable to get any direct feedback from the nurse in the Emergency Room. My daughter's phone was turned off. With the hazards lights on, my husband raced to the hospital. Even though my husband was speeding, the ride felt let an eternity. To keep from losing my mind, I prayed and prayed and prayed. As soon we made it to the hospital, we jumped out of the car and dashed to the ER.

Then, we were given the tragic news. Our beloved Cassidy Michelle had only lived a few minutes after being born. What we walked into we were not prepared for. My daughter and her husband were wailing. I could feel their deep hurt. Cassidy was in her crib. The nurses had dressed Cassidy, and my daughter wanted her nearby. She did not want to hold her, but I did. **Have you ever held a deceased grand baby or child?** *I hope not.* That was a defining moment for me. Because of faith, my family and I made it through this tragedy. From that moment on, I decided to live my life in a vastly different way.

Going through that trial taught me many lessons. Time does not stop. And if you want to do something, you have got to do it. Prior to that moment, I was playing in business but not taking it super seriously. I also realized that I was playing fearful, and my children were watching me be unhappy in corporate jobs and that I needed to step out and build my business now. It was time. So, I got my ducks in a row, hired an executive business coach and within a year, walked away from my corporate job. Today, I have the best JOB in the world, because I created it on my own terms.

Throughout the years, like any business Conglomerate Empowerment has had staffing, payroll, visibility, sales, etc. challenges. Our struggles in business have allowed us to investigate the root cause of the problem, test viable solutions and win again. Before COVID-19, my company landed a big corporate client. Unfortunately, at the start of the pandemic our client had to cancel their contract due to their limited funds. This was a major setback for our company. We had no time to worry. Our team still had clients to serve and bills to pay so we formed a strategic plan. At the onset, we started helping people start new businesses for free. Personally, I pivoted, hired a new executive business coach, and learned how to "really" conduct business online. I am proud to say that our company has grown during the pandemic

(Thank you God!). Every personal and business struggle we faced have turned into steppingstones towards our success.

Today, I confidently stand as a Boss Nana. I am unafraid. I know how to use my God-given gifts to create wealth and total life prosperity not only for myself, but for others. I am soaring in my gifts, and I absolutely love serving my clients and staff members. Encouraging/equipping business owners, paying business taxes, vacationing, and cooking homemade meals for my family is an honor. I am glad I said yes in 2009 and recommitted to my dream in 2015. I am a Boss Nana who chooses to live and soar by the Word of God.

Now is your turn:

1. What do you really want to do?
2. List 3 obstacles that is stopping you from living your ideal life and/or dreams?
3. Identify 3 solutions for each obstacle and then do them!

Connect with Dr. Tonya- Email answers to ceo@drtonyab.com

BIOGRAPHY: *Dr. Tonya Blackmon, aka "Queen of Grants," is a Highly Sought-After Transformational Global Speake/Trainer, Small Business Funding Expert, Mucho Dinero TV Show Executive Producer (#muchodinerotv), 2021 Black, Bold & Beautiful Girl Boss Honoree, and Super Proud "Boss Nana."*

She is a 3X Best-Seller/ 1X New Release Co-Author: (Pray, Slay and Collect, Boss Moms & International Women of Color who Boss Up, & Manifesting Excellence); Author: 7 Days Dive into Spiritual Success (#1 New Release) & Boss Nana - How to Actually Become One. Founder: Conglomerate Empowerment (CGE), TEK UP Academy, VP of 2Savage Magazine online and print. Connect with Dr. Tonya on Social Media https://linktr.ee/drtonyab7

2

"You too are a Star Valuable"

Amelia Starr

With a name like A. Starr, one may imagine a glamorous life, a life filled with glitz and stardom. "A Starr," seems as though it should be in flashing lights. Yes, I am A. Starr and truly it was predestined that I would illuminate the world. My story is not one of glitz or glamour, but ironically, it's one of trauma, resilience, perseverance, and tenacity.

I was born to a teenage mother with many ghosts of her own that haunted her. She was fighting her own demons when she birthed me. You see, my mother was addicted to drugs and the fast life surrounding being a teen addict. She found herself entangled with a much older man who forced her into prostitution. Once she became pregnant with me, her beloved pimp wanted nothing to do with her unless she'd chosen to abort. My mother refused to terminate her pregnancy. My dad's fury raged as he beat her, breaking several of her ribs. On the night of November 15, after years of suffering intense abuse on multiple levels with broken ribs, the labor pain began. The pain intensified then a rapid burst of warm water flowed down her legs. The pain from the broken ribs made pushing intolerable. As she lay in the hospital bed in agonizing pain I was born. I had passed my first cruel test of survival! My mother's last name was Corbett and my father's Stukes. It was that night that my mother named me Amelia Love Starr. Decades later when I asked why she didn't give me one of their last names. She grinned and said, "Well it was night and you, my darling, were and always will be my star!"

I didn't feel like a star. Mom gave me to her foster mother to raise when I was 2 years old. I understand this was done out of love. It was intended to provide me with more opportunities than she could give me. It was her ultimate sacrifice. This selfless decision caused me to question my self-worth and even my existence at a young age. Although in a loving home, I went through periods where I felt rejected, betrayed, and unworthy. I was embarrassed and hated my name as it reminded me, I had no identity. It was like I was wearing the scarlet letter A. Starr was no better, it was a name that no one else had and a constant reminder that I was different and did not belong. Little did I know God was preparing me to inspire others.

One morning before school, while listening to the radio to see if there was a snow delay in my quaint southern home a tune began to play. I became nauseated, yet I was not sick. I oddly hummed the tune to the song that I never remember hearing. Many years went by before I gained an understanding of why this song made me so nauseous. Once a teen I went to live with my mother in Pennsylvania. She became my best friend, like the big sister I never had.

On a summer day as my mother and I were out, she was reintroducing me to some of her friends. Instantly the song, heard so many years before, began to violently play in my mind as I stared into his eyes during the introduction. An unknown foul taste caused my mouth to water. I stood there paralyzed at 15 years old, as a movie began playing right before my eyes. I saw the dark gloomy room with light peeking through the dirty window shade. The song played louder and louder! The stench that filled the room as he coerced me to perform oral sex on him at two years old became so intense, I begin to violently vomit! The fear in his eyes confirmed that he knew just who I was and that I knew what he'd done. The confusion I felt provoked me to silence. Now I understand why the song made me so sick! I hated him, yet I never told. Since we did not live in the same neighborhood, I seldom saw him. I kept busy focusing on adapting to city life. I still wonder from time to time if I was given to him as payment for my mother's addiction? Did she know what he was doing to me? Is this why she sent me to the country to live?

Mom was abruptly snatched from this earthly realm. After my mother's departure I felt betrayed. There were so many unanswered questions. Other addicts were still alive and given another chance. They were enjoying their family and making memories, but that was over for me. My mom was forever gone. Once again, I feel that I got jaded by life! I was livid; God how could you take my only source of unconditional love, my cheerleader, my biggest fan? We were still making up for all the time we missed out on during my childhood. It's not fair! What were you thinking, now I have no one to rely on? Throughout life I have boxed with life, I'd taken blows, been knocked down but this was a knockout! I accomplished material things and was able to obtain possessions that others my age had not yet attained because I truly lived for the applause of my mom. How was I supposed to make it!

Shortly after my mother's death I fell into the trap of a narcissistic vulture preying on my vulnerabilities. He pretended to care and gained my trust. I transparently shared with him my deepest insecurities in confidence, trusting his empty promises of stability and security. Naive and lonely, I made the worst mistake of my life and married the enemy. Someone who hated my existence thrived on degrading me by discounting my accomplishments as if we were in competition. Then came the conspiring, manipulating, and controlling behaviors. I was blindsided when I was encouraged not to work and was prevented from having a true career as my main priority was to care for him. I was swindled out of my financial freedom first, which immediately made me dependent on him. The threats begin, "I can divorce you and you wouldn't know it until the military police knock on the door to remove you from housing," he gloated. I believed this for too many years. My biggest fear was of being homeless and he reminded me regularly that he could make it happen. Not only were finances utilized as a weapon of control, but I also had to beg for necessities for myself and my children. It just got worse as time went on, the financial abuse mutated into verbal accusations and threats. I was constantly belittled and berated in the home while smiling for the cameras of life and being showered with hush gifts. My heart was broken from the loss of my mother. I was devastated, and depressed at an all-time low, but that was not enough. Soon fights and choking became part of the routine, along with intimidation and mind games. There were fits of unwarranted anger and lack of self-control which spawned insurmountable amounts of fear. We walked on eggshells at home and tried to be in public as much as possible because in public he was the perfect gentleman. We appeared to be the perfect family.

One day I woke up from my real-life nightmare of sorts. I decided I had enough and planned my escape. I knew if I stayed, he would kill me! Finally, I saw the toxicity was beyond repair when multiple guns were brought into the home. This gun toting demon was brazen with his steel weapon. I was terrified at night. He warned me that he could kill me and get away with it because of his selective PTSD.

Lies were told, rumors started, but I focused on my purpose, my talents. I began to do what was necessary for the safety of myself and my children. **As the chains of bondage were being broken, I blossomed into A. Starr.** I am rebuilding and enjoying my newfound freedom. It is liberating to freely pursue my passions and encourage others to do likewise. I am no longer battling with feelings of fear and inadequacy, but shining brightly, encouraging others to boldly fulfill their destiny.

Life is simply a concoction of tribulation and triumph. If you get up more times than you fall, you'll always be triumphant. It may take you by surprise, true indeed, but it doesn't have to shock you into the pits of despair. Strive daily to be the best version of you, escape when necessary and survive... live your life unapologetically and illuminate your world.

You too are A. Star.

Shine Bright!

BIOGRAPHY: *A.Starr is an inspirational storyteller and published author of the award-winning memoir,* **The Many Facets of A Starr: Purifying Truths**. *As mother of three with an Associates of Arts in Communication, a Bachelor of Science in Business-Healthcare Management and a diploma in Practical Nursing, Amelia has enjoyed reading and writing literary works of all genres throughout her life. Over twenty years of writing experience was born from the many pathways she has voyaged throughout her life. Though her life has been riddled with uncertainty, rejection, violence, and death, it also has been a series of inconceivable triumphant moments. Amelia incessantly strives to shine bright being the best version of who God has destined her to be, A. Starr! Unapologetically, she lives a fruitful, abundant, and happy life. When not writing, Amelia can be found illuminating the world by serving and advocating for others. Additionally, she enjoys serene walks on the beach, meditation, and cozying up with a good book!*

3

It's Not the End; It's a New Beginning

Aretha Ford-Metts

"So many women live in silence within a marriage violated by the one who vowed before God, family and friends to cherish, love and honor. I knew this wasn't what God planned for my life nor what He had in mind when two become one in marriage."

How do you process the hurt from someone you loved so deeply and gave your all to building a future together? How do you recover from the gut wrenching screams and howls into a stack of pillows, so the household has no clue of the depth that your soul has been shaken? How is it possible another human being could cause such damage that you question who you are and whose you are? How could you not know; you never saw it coming, or did you? How do you overcome being MisHandled by loving someone else or lack of love for self? This could not be what God meant for marriage to be!

As I lay here 2 months shy of my 2nd year anniversary recovering from a stroke that resulted from years of me being the superwoman of all things: work, projects, family, friends, husband and all the weight of the world he poured on me both seen and unseen. I was never the superwoman for myself. This was my second stay in a hospital, my first stay was the birth of me. This one could have been the end, but it turned out to be the BEGINNING of ME!

Yes, I have loads of questions for my spouse: when, where, why and how. When did you and I lose the US? Where did our foundation begin to crack or was it ever strong? Why are we standing in this hurtful place now? Why didn't you say something beforehand? How do we mend these broken hearts? Or is it impossible to return to what we once had? On good days, I understand these questions may never get answered and I harden my heart, so I don't care (this isn't me) and drown myself in work. On those bad days I want answers so I call and text him or binge on TV when no solutions could be found. He has the answers to the puzzle. He knows where every piece goes, all the twists and turns, the dates and times, the other women, and dives. He holds the box top of the puzzle with the picture because this is his painting of chaos. I was given just enough pieces to keep me entertained, to post paintings of a perfect picture for the public eyes of those who didn't know of the behind the scenes lies. For those who knew, they smiled in my face and said to themselves, "this girl has no clue about her boo." No one was grown enough to be a friend, family, or husband to clue me in. But why should they? How could you not be keen on your own household and surroundings when deception is fed by the one you bed and believe. This is not crazy in love but just crazy!

As months pass, seasons change and I was still laying in puddles of tears wishing, hoping, and praying for the man I love, my knight of shining armor, would finally show up for me, for us. I was giving too much control to someone who wasn't concerned about the games they played on me, someone who never called to try to explain or fix the situations but cowardly moved on in life to the next person/s who excitedly gave them attention to their demands and requests. It was time for me to climb out of the hole I was dumped in because death hadn't taken me, but new life was rescuing me from the pit they dug for me. It's here in the "Bottom of the Barrel" a glimpse of light called my name, "My daughter Aretha, you have work to do!" Like the sermon my spiritual sister gave, while in the barrel the light is nurturing you. It's replaying times and events, places, and faces, decades of love, hurt, birth and deaths. It's rebirthing you with new strength, purpose, and new dreams but you must be willing and receiving to be purged.

What do I mean by purge? The purge is a climb through your tears of hurt, disappointment with them and yourself, abandonment, the loneliness, the why me, how could this be, the disrespect and much more. The answers I was looking for are not in a How-to book, but in the process. The answer to all the above questions and many more is part of your purging to your growth, your path, your light, your PUR-POSE. The process is the joy of coming out of the darkness, realizing your worthiness, that you build for LIFE and LOVE. The same love you give is the same love you're granted to have, but you must operate differently. You must be keen on your surroundings, spirits, sounds and signals.

My tears and frowns are replaced with lashes and smiles. My healing process is feeding my spirit with scripture, mediation, and sisters who have been MisHandled but healed completely. Married couples who suppress their flesh to walk in Kingdom married life with their spouse. Emotional therapy is my favorite daytime date. We pull back the layers to expose the dirt and cleanse the wound so mending can begin. I have a small circle of true loyal girlfriends (no Judas aloud) who I break bread with and feel safe. I still believe in pure love but always and forever self-love first. My anchor scripture is Psalms 71;18 *Now also when I am old and grey-headed, O God, forsake me not; until I have shewed thy strength unto this generation, and thy power to everyone that is to come.*

MisHandled is my podcast journal of the walk through my husband's lie's, deceit and betrayal: how the violations affected me Mentally, Physically and Spiritually. (The End) Real Talk With Aretha is my testimony of triumph over it all. You too can welcome your NEW BEGINNING! Annetta Barnes - Bottom of the Barrel sermon 2018 Bibleway COGIC Cincinnati, Ohio

BIOGRAPHY: *Aretha Ford-Metts is the podcast creator of MisHandled, her personal journal of spousal lies, deceit and betrayal; how the impact from these violations affects you Mentally, Physically and Spiritually. Aretha began healing herself from her own trauma by attending Emotional Polarity Technique Therapy with much success, she has started embarking on obtaining her Certifications as a Mindful Relationship and Life Coach. Real Talk with Aretha is a LIVE talk show once a week that addresses unspoken conversations that haven't taken place before, during and after marriage. Such topics - infidelity, swingers, STI, children outside the marriage, religion, divorce laws and so much more. This journey has opened doors to Aretha taking the stage as a Motivational/Spiritual Speaker at "I Love Me Conference" Cincinnati, Ohio, " Level Up Summit", Power Up Summit", "Come Back Champion Conference", an Ambassador for "A Queen's Round Table Symposium" and many more future events. By sharing her truth, connecting with the hearts of women to allow them to see they are not alone, "MisHandled is what happens to you but not who you are." Encouraging, enlightening, and helping women to evolve into finding their healing, their voice and G.L.O.W into their future.*

Contact email: aretha@mishandled.club

4

Returning to the Pledge Line: A Story of Overcoming Workplace Bullying

Barbara Floyd Jones (*MonumentMom*)

While there are Americans sounding the alarm about the mistreatment of Black people at the hands of Whites, I want my story to shine a light on women who experience bullying in corporate environments. For women of color, often, hazing is not committed by a White person, but by Black and Brown women that reflect their own skin tone. I have experienced first-hand workplace bullying.

According to a recent study conducted by The Workplace Bullying Institute, 65% of bullies are managers. Female bullies target other females 65% of the time, 43.2% of remote workers are bullied; and 76.3 million workers are affected by workplace bullying.

When I first experienced a bullying incident, I was quite surprised. The bully was a woman that I had worked with on several projects and appeared to work quite well with me. As a matter of fact, we had several personal conversations; exchanging pleasantries such as where we lived, went to school; and where we took our summer vacations. She was well-dressed, highly educated, and socially connected. We even shared several commonalities. On the surface it appeared we were on our way to a long journey of being comrades in the workplace. However, I was mistaken.

The first few microaggressions were very subtle. She would omit me from vital e-mail communications, provide information to my colleagues that should have been given to me; and turn down my requests to assist with projects. As time progressed, her behavior indicated she had no intention of authentically working with me, but against me.

Eventually, her subtleties became an outright disregard for my role as a project leader. She would often make it difficult for me to connect with her to obtain relevant information for my projects. She planted seeds of distrust and confusion when new employees joined the team; outright lied when asked about her knowledge pertaining to a project; and openly challenged and refuted my presentations during corporate meetings.

The more I tried to avoid meetings and events with her; the more I was tasked with working with her. For me, the career I loved became toxic. There were many days that I did not want to go to work. I asked my confidants (The Tribe) if there was something I could do to make the situation better. I received a mixed bag of advice including a justified beat down, ignoring her, filing a formal complaint, talking to my manager; and going to the EEOC. There was even a time when I thought I would resign, but just as quickly as the thought entered my head; it fled. And while each suggestion allowed me to mentally play out the scenario, I knew I would always take the high road. I was committed to my work, and no one had the power to force me to resign.

In some way, I believe she relished in her demonizing behavior. Besides diminishing my enthusiasm, the bully also lowered the morale of several staff members. The more this occurred in an open setting, the more aware I became that senior management was unwilling; or not capable of halting the bully's behavior.

To preserve my sanity, I submitted a complaint to my manager. Meetings were held, documents submitted, and at the end of the day very little changed internally. It was almost as if management was telling me that bullying was ok if the work was getting done. I had given up and succumbed to the resolution that this would be the new normal. Until one day I remembered that I loved who I was and the work I did. I no longer wanted to participate in a constant round of verbally being slapped and slapping back. I loved working with my team, and it was going to take God and The Line to elevate my mindset and response.

I took a few days off to step out of the situation: mentally and emotionally. I turned to God. He had been my anchor for many years. There was no doubt about his ability to help now. My other source of comfort and inspiration, The Line. Joining The Line for 90 days is how I pledged to become a member of a national sorority. In 1990, The Line was in Providence, Rhode Island with 9 women solely relying on one another. We were arm-to-arm and back-to-back. We met unreasonable demands, missed many hours of sleep, solved many riddle-laced assignments; and worked together to reach our goal.

The Line is where I learned that people would dislike me just because of my association. The Line is where I learned to persevere for long periods of time; and if I did get tired, my sisters would have my back. The Line is where I learned that in life there would be people who would heckle me and do things to try to get me to fail. The Line is where I learned that a woman holding her chin up and being silent created more attention and got more accomplished than the clanging brass sounding voice of her haters. The Line is where I learned a woman could achieve whatever she put her mind to, including dealing with insecure women.

I made it over that season of mental anguish. Through much prayer, rounds of talks with The Tribe, and my memories of The Line, I reclaimed the strength I needed when I thought about giving up. I reflected on The Line and how there were many times I thought it was a waste of time; just silly rituals girls created. Little did I know the life lessons it was preparing me for, those I would recall when I was being challenged beyond my own ability and reason.

My new mindset allowed me to realize I could only be disappointed when I had expectations for a person, they weren't capable of meeting. I started to look at my bully through a different lens. She was a miserable oppressor, inflicting discomfort on her colleagues. How terrible it must have felt to be her; to not even be aware nor care how ugly her behavior made her look. How insecure she must have been to constantly nitpick with me in meetings over every minutia; and rejecting my requests all under the guise of doing what is best for everyone. How tired she must have been with the constant struggle for power and control.

I am thankful to God for giving me the ability to endure. Endurance is not a skill I sought to improve, but I am forever grateful I could. I am relieved that my mental and emotional state has been restored. Most of all, I am appreciative of the experience of not only joining The Line but crossing over it.

BIOGRAPHY: *Barbara Floyd Jones, aka MonumentMom, is a Christian wife and mother who has embraced homeschool completely. She has a BS in Marketing and a MA in Public Administration. Over the span of her professional career, she has managed marketing campaigns with budgets of*

$6M+, conducted national and local media interviews and facilitated work-shops around the country on how to educate and engage local communities.

5

A New Dawn on Life's Horizon

Darshell Andrews

I lay in the corner, head throbbing as I attempt to open my swollen bloodshot eyes. Sunlight is peeking into the room, as he exits, slamming the door. My babies come out from hiding and run to my side. They were as helpless as I am. No words were said, we just held each other sobbing. It was like there was no way out. This seemed to be my portion and I simply could not fight fate.

How did we get here? This man was supposed to be my destiny. I dreamed of building with and growing old with him. He was attractive, funny, charming, and thoughtful. I felt protected and loved when we were together. I used to be cherished and showered with affection. The very thought of him would give me palpitations and make me smile. I was so proud to be his wife. One day I just wasn't enough. He began to come home later and later, tip toeing in with excuses. Eventually, he shamelessly flaunted his relationships with other women. I was devastated. I battled with feelings of depression and inadequacy. Somehow my prince, my hero, my husband had morphed into a monster with no soul.

Those once loving eyes filled with adoration had turned into pitch black evil. His terrifying glare stabbed me to my core as I trembled. Leaving was impossible, I had my girls to care for. I could not leave them behind, nor could I take them into a shelter and risk having them placed in foster care, or a possibly a worse situation. I begged for help from his chain of command. The military simulated an investigation to pacify me with no real intentions of helping. My case was prolonged as the beating became more frequent and more intense. Finally, it was crystal clear. My babies and I were simply a liability to the military. Their loyalty was with their soldiers!

Searching for help, clarity, and restoration, I turned to a local church. I had been victimized and abused in front of my daughters. I was naive and deceived as I transparently pleaded to church leadership. I needed more than religious rituals to practice. I truly needed a savior! My daughters and I had suffered in silence for years. When I'd finally decided to ask for guidance and was trying to get help, I was betrayed. It was the church who ridiculed and rejected us. What in the hell was going on? Feelings of abandonment and insignificance overcame me as

I was called into a small, cluttered office in the church's foyer. It was here I was notified that I had been barred from the church!

Emerging to consciousness, disorientated I lay in agonizing pain. My limp body is barely able to grip life. The smell of rotten food and feces invade my nostrils as I come to the realization I am behind a dumpster. With my purple bruised blood-stained hands, I attempt repeatedly to sit upright without success. I would plummet into a pool of my blood on the jagged asphalt. In the pit of despair, my mind raced realizing that I was thrown out like trash! Left for dead! Where were my girls? They need me. I couldn't help myself, much less of them. Tears begin to flood my face as I helplessly lay praying. Dear God, I need you! My daughters need you. HELP US NOW! Suddenly I heard the shrieking sound of breaks. I was found by an elderly woman in a powder blue sedan. She told me how she'd driven by many times and felt obligated to see where the blood was coming from. With tears in her eyes, she called for help and even stayed with me until emergency transport arrived.

Livid and recovering in my cold small hospital room, reality mentally whipped me into shape. Why was I in this predicament? It was at this moment of self-reflection a shift happened as I saw my dawn approaching. I mustered up the energy to call my sister. "Darshell!" she cried, "Where are you?" A tear-filled conversation informed me that my girls were safe and with their Auntie. They called her after being left home alone without being able to reach me. My heart was full, my babies were safe, God had answered my prayers.

Day by day I regained my strength. Mentally and physically, I was growing and getting stronger. I was given a second chance in life, and I was ready to live it. No longer was I going to accept any type of abuse, for I now see I have purpose. While in recovery, local police interviewed me in the hospital. Child protective service interviewed my daughters. After discharge from hospital, doors of opportunity began to slowly open for me. I accepted a job in health, education and wellness which required me to relocate. With my sister agreeing to care for my daughters, I packed my belongings up in my car and eagerly set off to make a new beginning for us all.

I had nothing but what was in my car. I could not afford housing and so each night after work I discreetly slept in my car in their garage. Every morning, I would go to the gym. There I showered, got dressed, and then drove back to and parked in the garage. Then I proceeded into work with a smile. Despite being homeless, I was happy! I was able to experience stolen freedoms that I had forgotten existed. This work experience was therapeutic, as I enjoyed helping others at work. Seemly work sped up my healing process. In practically no time I was able to obtain housing and reunite with my daughters. Also, I enjoy seeing others thrive, so I accepted an additional opportunity to advocate for students in alternative schools. Life was good and getting better! As for the ex, justice was finally somewhat served. He is in prison and unable to hinder or wreak havoc in our lives.

Meanwhile, I befriended a beautiful soul who made mouth-watering desserts. She inspired me into entrepreneurship. After complaining about a less than pleasing potato I had gotten at a local diner, Taste Budz was birthed. We started in a ghost kitchen, offering pick up, conduct and delivery of a variety of entrees served inside a scrumptious potato. Now, we have grown into a dine-in restaurant! As I continue to grow and heal, I encourage you to follow your dreams as your dawn is coming!

6

When the PREY Began to PRAY

Dr. Carolyn Stephens

"Become the change you desire to see" -Ghandi

It is my prayer that as you read this chapter, that you receive the level of healing that you need to make this journey to get over to the other side. I cannot tell you what is on the "other side" but; what I can say to you is that wherever you are in your life right now, there is an "other side" for you! As you read this you may have your bags packed and ready to travel over to the "other side". I believe that you can feel in your spirit right now that there is something else for you. I also believe that your spirit senses that everything you have endured and encountered has prepared you for your next level. I believe that you are sensing that you are about to arrive at a place where your divine purpose and destiny are about to come together. I would encourage you to "travel light"! I encourage you to travel light because naturally most women have the tendency, including myself, tend to overpack. I believe that we overpack because we are afraid that when we arrive at our destinations, we won't have all that we need to enjoy our destination. I would admonish you, that for where you are going you will need to leave all the emotional baggage you have acquired behind you! You will only need to reserve the memory of what you have packed in those bags as a reminder of the strength and wisdom that you have acquired during this journey called life. I believe that when you arrive at the place of your next level that you will begin to reflect upon the words of the old hymnal "My soul looks back and wonder ...how I got over"

How did I make it over? There have been many people who held my hand and strengthened me, encouraged me, taught me, cried with me, and fought with me to assist me through my pain and I am forever thankful for each of them. During the times in my life where I felt most vulnerable and bathed in the tears of my pain... the one journey tool that has provided me with the strength that I have needed to make it over to the other side is PRAYER.

When I was invited to participate in this project, I asked the creator to provide me with a title...and the word "prey" came to my spirit. I am somewhat familiar with the term prey however being a city girl I had to resort to the dictionary to provide myself with a formal definition of the word prey to receive a deeper understanding of why

I was given this title. The word prey means..."an animal that is hunted and killed by another for food"

There were many times in my life where I was as naïve as a small child when it came to engaging in various relationships in my life. For the most part I have always been very trusting and very loving, always focusing on the good in people. As a very young girl my mother would often say..." Carolyn, everybody is not your friend!". I would become so confused when she would say that and found it hard to believe that the girls in the school yard of P.S. 15...the elementary school that I attended in Brooklyn were not my friends. Surely my mother was wrong about the girls that I shared my candy and potato chips with. They were not only my friends...but my best friends. My mother certainly was wrong about my Highschool friends who I cut school with to smoke weed with on Fridays were my friends. I even thought she was wrong about my girlfriends who I hung out with in Coffee Park listening to music with and going to parties and getting on the dance floor to do the current dance move at that time which was called the "Hustle" were my friends. What in the world did she mean when she said, "Everybody is not your friend?!". I lived in this world of innocence of thinking, always believing in the good of mankind, and I still truly believe in the divine good of mankind and it is that belief that continues to give me hope that all people can be better and do better if they so choose.

It wasn't until I entered young adulthood that I fully understood the pain that people could inflict upon the heart. When I first arrived in Atlanta, Ga some 30 years ago and thought I would go for a walk in Downtown Atlanta only to be raped violently in an unconstructed park, that; I realized how truly cruel people could be. I became acquainted with deep pain when I was choked and kicked down on my kitchen floor while I was pregnant with my son David, and I realized that some men could inflict a level of pain on a woman that is almost unspeakable. I thought as many good-hearted people do, that I would escape or somehow subvert the level of pain that I had endured by fully submerging myself in the church and the workings of church ministry. I thought to myself "Now surely I would be safe in the church" a place where I just knew people would be kinder, gentler, and would ease the pain of my wounded heart. As I found my place in ministry not fully understanding my call, I found myself preaching aggressively and doing my version of what I felt was the work of the Kingdom only to face a different kind of pain.

Once again, oftentimes my childlike thinking kicked in and I felt that loving people would bring me the love I so earnestly desired and longed for. Surely the "preacher man" and the "preacher woman" would love me and nourish the spiritual giftings that God had placed upon my life. As I made my home among the people in the pews only to be kicked out of the church where I had placed my whole heart and clung to the words that exuded out of the Pastor's mouth. When I was kicked out of the church and was told 'You preach too loud" or "My people are following you and not me" I found myself once again rejected, betrayed, and confused. While out in the wilderness as I called it, I had become a spiritual foster child who had no home, I encountered more pain through the violent words of people who acted as if though they despised me, yet at the same time I was embraced by people who loved my giftings. The years that followed I endured levels and levels of heartache from various relationships that I had been in with men who I thought truly loved me just for me. I encountered people who came in my life as thieves in the night to steal my ideas, plunder my gifts, prostitute my potential, and beat me into submission so they could bask in a false sense of power.

When I turned 40 years old, my father told me a story about my childhood. It was years before I could understand why he chose to tell me that story at that juncture of my life. My dad told me that when I was just an infant he and my mother lived on Saratoga Ave. in a 3-story apartment in Brooklyn. My father told me that when I was a newborn that I used to cry uncontrollably, and it unnerved my mother to the point that the only way she felt she could find relief was to throw me out of a window. My father told me that, out of nowhere, as my small infant body was falling from that three-story window that there just happened to be a man who was walking by, and he stretched out his arms and caught me. Now I want to say that I had never revealed to my beloved departed mother what my father had shared with me. I have never held bitter feelings against my mother because; I learned as a mental health professional that my mother had a condition called postpartum depression.

However, it was at that time of my life that a question that I had long held in the chambers of my heart began to slowly begin to be answered. **I had often asked "God Why have people rejected me so, why have men abused me both physically and emotionally yet they claimed they needed me in their lives?"** Why when in the darkest moments of my rejection did people only enter my life as vultures to feast on the carcass of my rejected soul? these were always questions I found no answers for. They wiped off the forks and knives as they feasted on the ideas that I had put on their plates and satisfied their greedy natures. However, even during the times when I felt most rejected, I would always find peace in the one place I knew was home and that was the place called PRAYER.

For me PRAYER was not something that I did, but when I received a deeper meaning of Psalm 91 "He who dwells in the secret place of the highest shall abide under the shadow of the almighty..." **I found a place in prayer.** When my body was bloody and beaten from the abuse, I endured from men I found solace in this place called PRAYER. I share this piece of my life because I want you Queens who read this chapter to understand who you are! *I want you to know that Queen you were not rejected because something is wrong with you, however everything is marvelously right with you Beautiful Queen!* I realized much like the deer who gets shot down in the forest by the hunter with the gun, that I had served as prey for many of these people who came into my life with their guns to shoot me down. I realized that like the purpose that the prey serves that I was only the food that many of these people needed, and they ate sumptuously off the love, the generosity, the creativity that I provided for them.

However, my dear Queen sisters I in that moment realized

how powerful of a being I was this divine vessel called Carolyn who once was PREY began to PRAY! I realized that my life was profound, and I was divinely appointed by God. I began to accept that this anointing that God had placed on my life was here to serve and to be used by him to help set the captives free. I realized that because of who I was that I would be a terror to the enemy. I realized that though the gifting in my life would bring comfort to many people but simultaneously it would threaten many people. I want to share with you what I discovered...so that you know that all the pain you have endured in your lifetime was because when the heavens spewed you out into the earth realm through your mother's womb, you would be a beautiful gift to many people. Your special kind of style, walk, speech makes you the divinely authentic being that you are, and no one can reach people, teach people, empower people, the way you do. I know I am speaking to many of you beautiful queens who have been marred and scarred by life. I know that many of you have been victimized and rejected by the vultures and many of you have often thought you were left for dead.

I tell you through this chapter of the book...you have the power in you to overcome every obstacle and the pain of rejection and betrayal. You will and are now crossing over to the other side.

It is imperative for this next move in your life my sisters that **YOU PRAY!** Not looking at prayer as a verb just as something that you do but know that you allow prayer to be a place where you find your peace. When you dwell in that place, that metaphysical place called prayer you will always make it over. Prayer will carry you as it has done for me to places in the realm of the spirit where you will find victory every time.

How did I make it over? I made it over WHEN THE PREY PRAYED! PEACE AND BLESSINGS TO YOU MY BELOVED QUEEN SISTERS!

BIOGRAPHY: *Dr. Carolyn Stephens was raised in NYC. Dr. Carolyn now serves as a community clinical therapist and a family support specialist. She also holds a Doctorate in Divinity and Theology. She uses her education* and experience to promote cultural diversity with a focus on empowering and developing African American women. Currently, she serves as the CEO of Blackhouse Collaborations LLC. and is the visionary of the" I Am a Black Woman" and the "I Am A Black Man" book series. Dr. Carolyn also serves as the CEO of the Blackhouse Media Group and is a sought-after public speaker. She empowers women to rise above challenges and champion community strength through unification.

7

Storytelling Eases Life's Inevitable Pains

By Dr. Dawn Menge

All have a story to tell about our lives. Each one of us has overcome incredible obstacles to be where we are and who we are. Life is made up of victories and defeats. I am here to share just a little bit about those struggles and what I did with the bricks that were thrown at me. Dating has always been such a traumatic experience for me.

Growing up in a small town there weren't many dating opportunities. I was sixteen and our graduating class only held 80 people. My friends and I were out exploring the local mountains one night and ran across a group of new boys. We were having such a great time getting to know each other, but it was time to go home. I sat in front of my best friend's house talking with the boys until her father came out to the car, "It's time for you to go home your mom is calling us!" Oh my, was I in big trouble. The boy walked me to my door and my dad walked out from under the stairs telling him to go home and I was grounded for life. (Two weeks seemed like a lifetime at the tender age of sixteen).

Being grounded at sixteen is so heart wrenching. You think the whole world is having this amazing time and you aren't included. It goes very slowly. It was Thanksgiving weekend and I had used my persuasive powers to convince my parents it was imperative that I go on a double date with the boys we'd met and my best friend. Due to health issues my father had temporarily relocated us to a beach community, and they were feeling unhappy about moving me around in my junior year, so they very reluctantly agreed.

The big night came, and this boy very bravely shook my dad's hand. The boy seemed a little off, but we were allowed to go to a drive-in movie about an hour away. His driving was sporadic, so I scooched close to him, and he let me take the wheel. We were driving through the desert, and it was pitch dark. That's when my whole life was changed in an instant.

Coming up over a dip in the road, the headlights suddenly showed on a car stopped in the middle of the road. It was like a ghost car presenting doom to our young lives. I grabbed the wheel and turned it hard to the left only to be met with bright headlights from an oncoming car. Not knowing what else to do I let go of the wheel, we were catapulted into the ghost like car! You could hear tires screeching, metal crunching and blood curdling screams from my best friend behind me.

Then there was total silence. The boy next to me opened his car door and fell out. I could hear my best friend crying in the background and I looked down and all I could see was my thigh. I knew my leg was broken but it was trapped under the engine that had been pushed back by the impact. People were walking around the car, and I heard a man say there was gas leaking as he lit a cigarette. I screamed at him to put it out.

There were sirens and flashing red lights invading my semi consciousness. The fireman pulled me out as I screamed in his ear. At first the impact had numbed me but now I could feel the pain of my broken bones. In the emergency room they couldn't get hold of my parents as they tried to work on me. Finally, when what seemed like days but was only hours they appeared, scared and hurt. My mom picked the glass up off my body. They began to treat me and help me with the pain of a broken femur, cracked pelvis and sternum. I was finally able to get some rest.

What is that drilling noise? I looked down and they were using a drill to put pins in my leg to put me in traction for six weeks. I was not leaving the hospital for quite some time. During those long weeks, I started out pleasant and positive. The nurse told me it would not last, and she was correct. Within a week I became inconsolable, I wanted out. I would call my family begging them to let me go home. I stopped eating the hospital food. Three days of it is more than enough but six weeks at sixteen? My parents would come to visit me each day and bring me a hamburger to help me keep my strength up. My little brother would only be allowed to come to the window to see me. I learned to crochet and thankfully I loved to read. We were told that the man in the stopped car had been drunk and it was not his first time. He had disappeared and could not be held responsible. They were unsure if I would be able to have children due to the damage to my pelvis. My best friend had broken her cheekbone and had to have reconstructive surgery.

I spent the remainder of my junior year in high school recovering in various versions of body casts. I finally returned the last few weeks on crutches. I continued to date the boy I'd been with while I was in the hospital, and he was very supportive. After about six months we broke up but remained friends for a while.

My senior year was filled with snow skiing, dances, schoolwork, and teenage antics. Graduation night was spent at Disneyland and our ceremony was small but memorable. I soon became a fireman for the forest service in the Young Adult Conservation Corp and then continued as a cook for a local camp. I started training as a medical secretary to build my employment.

My best friend and I were cruising a local hang out called E street. Just like in the movies we drove up and down the street laughing, flirting with the boys and having a great time. Suddenly, a man all dressed in white drove by me on a motorcycle. He slowed as he passed us and asked us to pull over. We did and he stuck his head in the sunroof and asked me, "Where have you been all my life?" It was so corny, but he certainly caught my attention. He was handsome, sexy, a grown man of twenty-two and lived on his own. Within six months we were married. It was a beautiful wedding in an old mansion in an orange tree grove. We soon had three beautiful children, two girls and one boy. I was a stay-at-home mom and he worked hard to provide for us. Having children was a miracle after my accident and I devoted all my energy into raising them. In high school I had the dream that I would never be a stay-at-home mom. I was going to be a businesswoman. That thought became a memory as soon as I became pregnant. I was exactly where I wanted to be, and I've never regretted that decision.

We were married almost thirty years. But things began to change as our children became teenagers. He was gone a lot as a wildland firefighter, and we drifted apart. The red flags that I hadn't acknowledged about domestic abuse in his family began to emerge. Our relationship became more and more antagonistic. It increased to the point that I had to have him arrested and our marriage ended. I had graduated from college with my master's and credential and had been teaching students with severe cognitive delays for several years at that point. I think part of our downfall was my professional growth and increase in income. The dynamics of our relationship changed drastically, and he was no longer the sole breadwinner.

With my newfound single hood and empty nest, I was faced with a new life. Dating and rebuilding my life and what direction I wanted to take, I no longer needed to worry about my family and could just concentrate on myself. I began my PHD program in Curriculum and Instruction and started publishing my children's books. I loved to travel and wanted to share this with the world. It was a great outlet for me to have a new adventure to look forward to and my author journey created new experiences and meeting so many wonderful people. It took seven years, but I completed my PHD program and became Dr. Dawn Menge and have since published fourteen children's books and won over forty-one awards including recently several from film festivals in Vegas. Queen Vernita's Visitors educational adventure series won the Special Recognition Champion Award and Dragon's Breath won best book in the Miracle Makers film festival. What a journey my author path has taken me on. Book reviewer for a Children's magazine, literary judge for children's literature and indie romance, countless in person book events and interviews around the world. It's been a path of hard work, dedication and exploration. My traveling adventures have taken me around the world to swim with sharks, manta rays, turtles, hold baby alligators and kayak to glaciers and the La Bufadora.

Dragon's Breath is not part of the Queen Vernita series. It is a tale based on my experiences being harassed and stalked inside of my own home by a woman who did not want me dating a man who cared deeply for me. She came to visit saying she was part of a woman's ministry and could help me with my anxiety over my ex-husband. She spent most of the time trying to get information about this man and at the end told me, "He wanted a Dragon Slayer who was sexy, and she would never let it happen!" She told me that she had been reading her bible and God told her to come to my house in the middle of the night. She had been sitting in front of my house and said she saw a black cloud looking over my house and put a line of God's blood around my house. This of course was hogwash and she'd simply been looking for this man.

I had given her a set of my books for her grandchildren, and she snarled at me and asked what she was going to do with these books.

Not needing to be confrontational with a total stranger who I thought I'd never see again, I thanked her for her time and escorted her out. That was the beginning of six years of vandalism, gaslighting, and terrorizing me in my home to the point I was forced to sell it. She attempted to get me fired, and even was able to hack my emails to send letters to this man from me about fake conversations between us.

My friend and coworker were a great support through all of this, and we were sitting in the Sheriff's office trying to get help. The detective told me that it was this woman doing this and he tried very hard to find a way to prosecute her. But I'd already sold my house and was exhausted at that point. We took a trip to Vegas and created Dragon's Breath on the drive. When I got there, I called this man and read the story to him. He is the one who titled it Dragon's Breath. It's a story teaching kindness and empathy. Teaching children that it isn't ok to hurt people when you are angry or feeling jealous. It's won over six awards already and has been read all over the world.

I have moved my negative experiences into positive avenues to help children learn to deal and cope with life's inevitable pains. I have turned my family adventures into teaching tools for families to learn about true friendship, education, adventure, exploration, empathy, and kindness. Life is truly special.

BIOGRAPHY: *Dr. Dawn Menge has won over forty-one international awards as the author of the Queen Vernita educational series including the Special Recognition Champion Award from conquering disabilities with film festival. She holds a PhD in Curriculum and Instruction, a Master's degree and a Clear Credential in moderate/severe disabilities, and a Bachelor's Degree in human development. Dr. Menge has been Teaching students with severe cognitive delays for over twenty years. She has three children and six beautiful grandchildren and lives in Southern California.*

Queen Vernita's Visitors educational adventure series **http://www.drawnmenge.com**

8

How I Made It Over: 'On the Wings of Prayer'

Dr. Stacy L. Henderson

"Confess your faults one to another, and pray one for another, that ye may be healed.

The effectual fervent prayer of a righteous man availeth much." James 5:16 KJV

There is a phrase, "You're making on the wings of someone else's prayers" that has resonated with me for as long as I can remember. It references how oftentimes in life; we have a prayer life that leaves much to be desired. In other words, we do not talk with God as often as we should. Therefore, others pray on our behalf. From a personal point of view, prayer keeps the lines of communication open and helps to keep me in a right relationship with God. I admit that there were times when I was too discouraged or so upset that I refused to pray. Why? I doubted what God was doing in my life because I simply did not understand His plan or my purpose. I was immature in my faith - 'a babe in Christ' - as some might say. I had so much growing to do and throughout the process, I continuously fell short of the Glory of God. My relationship with Him was not being nurtured, mainly because I was not communicating effectively, nor did I have realistic expectations. For instance, when I would pray and the outcome was not as I desired or would have liked, I was disappointed. Or, when it seemed that the answers to my prayers were not provided quickly enough, I became doubtful. My prayer life needed 'spiritual reconstruction.' That is where the fight of the 'Prayer Warriors' came into play.

My mother, Mary, has always been the strongest woman I have ever known. No matter what the situation was she would always say, "Give it to God because he can do more with it than you can." Whether it concerned my struggles with self-esteem, performance in school, family relations or career matters - she always referred me to God. Sure, she would offer some anecdotal advice in the form of a story, reference a bible passage or parable, or cite a Gullah Geechee saying or an old wives' tale. But she stood on God's Word. She was a good listener with strong shoulders and a heart full of compassion. She shared her personal life experiences, and her level of transparency was forthright. She did not sugar coat anything nor did she water it down to make it easier to accept. She told it like it was. In any event, all roads led to God. Prayer was always her first line of defense against the strongholds of life. One passage she would quote is very simple, 1 Thessalonians 5:17: "Pray without ceasing." Yes. It is just that simple.

She would even give instructions on how to pray: Spirit-led, in a quiet place, humble, honest and with great expectancy.

I remember there was a time I was in much despair over a situation in my life. I confessed to her that I was so upset with God that I was not speaking to Him and refused to pray. She laughed and said, "You better hope that God never stops speaking to you. Stacy, life is not just about you - it is also about His purpose for you. You are blessed beyond measure to be a blessing to others. To whom much is given, much is required (Luke 12:48). You must grow in Grace, and it does not happen overnight. Allow God to work in you so that His purpose and calling on your life will become clear. I know it seems troubling and you don't have all the answers, but you will understand it better by and by. Everything happens in God's timing, not ours. But in the meantime, as you go through life, pray without ceasing. Seek His guidance, trust His promises and stand on His Word. And when you don't feel like praying, because as you say - 'You're not speaking to God' - always know that others are praying for you - especially me. Your father is in constant prayer because he listens closely when you talk about all your BIG dreams about doing your part to change the world and make it a better place. Your grandparents prayed that you would realize your calling and accept it. Although it would be challenging, it would be worth it because your Gifts are from God and must be used for the advancement of His Kingdom. Jesus prays for you because even He knows you have no idea what to pray for. So, he stands in the gap and prays to God on your behalf. You must have faith and put your trust in God. Just trust Him. I love you." Her words still give me comfort. Even to this day, I recall them to memory and keep them close to heart. Her lectures were filled with love.

Honestly, doing a heartfelt self-inventory was not easy but it was necessary. But once I sought the Holy Spirit for guidance, I was set on a course of intentionally seeking God. And although He already knew my heart, it felt good to openly identify and acknowledge my short-comings to Him. As I worked through the process, I discovered that my connection with God was built on an intellectual basis rather than on a personal one. It was not enough that I was reading and studying His Word; I needed to interact with Him on another level to experience a relationship in another realm. My devotion needed to evolve into a new dimension.

As time passed, I learned that by strengthening my bond with the Lord, I enjoyed a deeper sense of fulfillment. My mind was renewed, and my heart became more receptive to His purpose for my life. As a result, it was easier for me to face the adversities that came along with accepting my life's calling and walking in Godly Authority. My ears became more in tune to His Word which heightened my sense of discernment. My spiritual eyes allowed me to see the vision that God has for me from a new perspective. True intimacy with God was essential for strengthening our relationship. The quieter, quality time we spent in fellowship with one another, the deeper I delved into His Word. And I went from reading and studying His Word to taking it further by meditating on it and applying it to my life. Those revelations along my journey of 'divine connection' shifted my spiritual mindset, which greatly enhanced my prayer life and drew me closer to God. *"The Lord is nigh unto all of them that call upon him, to all that call upon him in truth"* - Psalm 145:18 KJV

Today, as I reflect over those times, I realize and confess that when going through the trials of life, it is a blessing to have those with Godly discernment and walking a Christian walk to pray for me. Although I did not see it then, I clearly see it now; their prayers comforted me in times of sorrow, shielded me when I was in danger and even encouraged me when things were going well. Bear in mind the words of John 17:20-23 KJV: *"20 Neither pray I for these alone, but for them also which shall believe on me through their word; 21 That they all may be one; as thou, Father, art in me, and I in thee, that they also may be one in us: that the world may believe that thou hast sent me. 22 And the glory which thou gavest me I have given them; that they may be one, even as we are one 23 I in them, and thou in me, that they may be made perfect in one; and that the world may know that thou hast sent me, and hast loved them, as thou hast loved me.*

So, when I look back over my life and reflect on my journey to share with you 'How I Made It Over,' I can truly say it has been on the wings of prayer. To God Be the Glory!

BIOGRAPHY: *Dr. Stacy L. Henderson, a native of Savannah, Georgia, is a retired Naval Officer with over 25 years of military service and experience. She is a Christian Educator, Inspirational Speaker, Businesswoman and an International Best-Selling Author. She speaks four languages and has publications in more than 40 language translations - two of which are in the White House Library. Her 'Stacy's Stocking Stuffer's' Christmas Charity has provided toys, meals, coats, clothing, and monetary support for families around the world since 1991. She has countless military and civilian accolades. Stacy is a domestic abuse survivor turned advocate who shares her life experiences and relies on faith-based doctrines to motivate and inspire others to achieve their best mental, physical and spiritual health. She is a Dean of Christian Leadership Schools at Christ Temple Baptist Church, Markham, Illinois and maintains close ties with her lifelong Church Family at Little Bryan Baptist Church, Savannah, Georgia. She has Degrees in Education, Health Services Management, Christian Leadership and Business Administration. A Proverbs 31 Woman, she utilizes her Spiritual Gifts to glorify God and edify His people. She is a loving Wife, proud Mother of two adult children (KeiSha and William) and several bonus children, and a doting Grandmother - comprising a blessed and beautiful 'Blended and Extended' Family. To God be the Glory!*

9

Trapped by Time

By Dr. Lovella Mogere

The conscious mind of the creator up-rises in every generation. The mind revolts, breaks and severs the restraints of mediocrity placed on His history makers over time. It is man's ideologies and cultural diffusion that contends against the universe's principles that legally and systematically desensitize mankind, causing them to plummet from their ascended state, thereby breaking the social order of the Creator.

Mediocrity, at its best, presents itself as a multiFACEted mask disguising, insignificant, lack of identity, utter nothingness. Once awakened, the menial state of one's awareness and existence reveal the Creator's original intent.

Your Significance

We are a people desperate for significance. Our determination to pursue life's purpose has been etched in our spirit from the beginning of time. This search propels us forward, making us breathless for power, having a driving desire to have our voices heard. Though our voices echo, some voices **resonate throughout time, making HIStory**.

The search for significance drives us. While in pursuit, some strive to control all aspects of their lives, whereas others obtain certainty by giving up control and adopting a philosophy of faith - a belief that one's life has meaning and importance. Some individuals will pursue this need by competing with others, or by destroying and tearing down those around them. However, others may endeavor to fulfill this need through connection with other human beings.

Life is the force for fulfillment. Fulfillment can only be achieved through a pattern of living focused on two needs: 1) Continuous growth (*evolution*) and 2) contributing beyond ourselves in a meaningful way (*revolution*). As humans empty, we continually make attempts to reach fulfillment of life's purpose. If we fail, we will settle for a comforter for meeting our needs on a small scale.

The Diffusion of Paradigm

Ideas as conceptions require compatible "mental sockets" in order to be interpreted by the adopter. That is, ideas need to be built on previously incorporated ideas to spread from one individual to another and, by extension, one society to another. Furthermore, individual ideas can be "assembled" into coherent blocks to be better exported, understood or simply to be more complex. The initial concepts of the diffusion of paradigms are to program society for systematic thinking.

For centuries, philosophical spheres (*influence*) proposed frameworks for examining the diffusion of paradigms. Prior to introducing the framework, ideologists reviewed relevant studies for a transformative movement of revolution (*change*), modifying the system at hand. These systems served as the basis for our differentiation between command (*order*) and demands (*economic process*). I propose seven classes of motivations, named commands. These are Government, Business, Family, Religion, Education, Arts and Entertainment, and Media. Each refers to the innovative and adaptive preferences of institutions where men seek to innovate in world systematic governance.

Trapped By Time

One trapped by time, slipstreams through decades, waits for the moment of their announcement according to the Creator's timetable. Romans 8:19 *"For the creation waits in eager expectation for the children of God to be revealed."* James A Baldwin said, *"People are trapped in history and history is trapped in them."* Those marked with distinction; signify the Creator's plans for humanity as HIStory, as it is made according to His plan. As the hearts of man are in sync with the Creator, false imaginations are cast down. One by one they surrender, thus redeeming time and fulfilling destiny.

It is the lost souls that are spiritually adrift that travel streamlines through timelines that positively disrupts a period of time, overturning outdated methodologies and systems seeking to execute the Creator's spiritual principles. The Creator will use whom He will, much like He used Apostle Paul to infiltrate and overthrow a pagan system and Mandela to rebuild and unite a nation that discriminated against his own people. They both desired to change the world. They were revered, groomed, and educated by a system that stripped their identity. And both found themselves overturning a system that actually reinvented them.

Time Seeks Opportunities to Showcase Dreams

Dreams, impregnated from eternity, come into reality once they are inspired or evoked. Dreams, as a power source, thrust one forward into time to mastermind, implement and execute a dream into reality. Life's turn of events, whether bitter or sweet, position or place one into a birthing position encircled by midwives (mentors).

Eventually, one realizes that through this, the Creator has presented an opportunity to showcase you. I dare you to become a protector of your dreams, a protector of your destiny. Break the self-imposed limitations, break the restraints of mediocrity and become the mind of God that defies time.

The question.. how I made it over?

Know this! The search for significance is overrated, while one seeks pleasure and lasciviousness methods to fill a void. Without identity, one could easily deny self (*purpose*) and forfeit destiny. It is known that throughout centuries that philosophies created cultures, social orders and built kingdoms (*spheres*) in hopes of duplicating God's Kingdom (realm). It is not by happenstance that the universe calls forth destiny - YOU, to advance the Creator's intent (*agenda*) through YOU. It is you, that the creator chose to bring reformation, revelation, and advancements to His kingdom (*realm*) on earth. God chose you to illustrate His thoughts and manifest His mind by defying time. You were chosen from the beginning of time, to allow your intelligence to defy what comes to kill, steal, and destroy your significance. Become the protector of your destiny.

BIOGRAPHY: *Dr. Lovella Mogere is the founder and president of Surge Hub, dedicated to helping Marketplace Leaders globally. She is a #1 best-selling author, motivational speaker and CEO of Nous Mass Media - "Raising the Levels of Consciousness and Intelligence" by providing a literary platform for authors globally. Lovella's ministry is dedicated to teaching biblical realities and kingdom principles to leaders building, shifting, transitioning and advancing through prayer. To learn more about Dr. Lovella Mogere visit www.lovellamogere.com*

10

Between Anticipation and Manifestation

"Vision without a plan, is just a pipe-dream."
Dr. Sanja Rickette Stinson

"Now faith is the substance of things hoped for, the evidence of things not seen." (Heb 11:1)

What do you do when God is silent? What do you do when God stops speaking after He has given you a foretaste of things to come? How do you handle the silence of God when you are ready to move forward, prepared to serve God, and eager to do God's will? What do you do when you are at the height of anticipation about what God is doing in your life and the life of your ministry, but you have yet to experience its full manifestation?

A period of silence is not new for God. Between the Old and the New Testament, God was silent for four hundred years. The Bible tells us that God's people waited to hear the voice of God

and for the manifestation of His promises. What an impenetrable thought to comprehend—to wait four hundred years in anticipation of the promises to be fully manifested.

After the people witnessed miracles—the spreading of the Red Sea, the prophets rising to bring forth His word—and after they witnessed God's sovereignty, they were awaiting His promise; God's people anticipated experiencing the full manifestation of the promises yet to come.

Why, now, was God silent for four hundred years? Why did God not reveal the purpose and direction to the people? Some scholars believe that during this historical Biblical time, there was a shift or pivot into a new dispensation called "grace." Nevertheless, waiting for and learning to trust God are crucial components when we are between anticipation and manifestation. God does not always unfold everything at once to us, and we must learn to wait.

Let's briefly examine some definitions of anticipation. Anticipation is a visualization of future events. Merriam–Webster's Collegiate Dictionary defines anticipation as "The act of looking forward; a picturing beforehand of future events."

As servant vessels of God, we must first remember that when God has us between anticipation and manifestation, "We walk by faith and not by sight." The Apostle Paul teaches that we are to continue to trust God for things that are unseen. Here is where our anticipation meets the unseen things that faith teaches us to hold on to and teaches us to trust God.

God sometimes keeps us in a holding pattern. This is the place or the position where we are caught between knowing what God is doing and actually seeing its manifestation. I believe that the holding pattern is where we often experience a heightened level of frustration. Such frustration causes us to get ahead of God's plans for our lives and derail our purpose.

"Be anxious for nothing, but in everything by prayer and supplication, with thanksgiving, let your requests be made known to God" (Philippians 4:7, KJV).

As people of God, the question might be how we deal with frustration when it meets anticipation. Naturally, the timing between frustration and anticipation seems longer, and waiting for God becomes more difficult. Timing is important in God's actions. Many lessons can be learned when we move too fast or get ahead of God's timing. Our response is to be anxious for nothing and to give thanks in advance of what has yet to manifest. We serve a God that keeps His promises! We should seek to nourish our anticipation with praise, prayer, and thanksgiving while waiting for the full manifestation of God's promises.

As life progresses, everyone experiences periods of anticipation. Personally, I've learned that even when God unveils His purpose. Anticipation is about positions and placements. A holding pattern represents a season of growth.

I believe this is a place or position where God is still refining, processing, and preparing us for something greater. God knows when we are ready for the next level: *"For I know the plans I have for you,' declares the Lord, 'plans to prosper you and not to harm you, plans to give us a hope and a future'"* (Jeremiah 29:11, NIV)

Nothing catches God by surprise, and nothing just happens. We serve a God who is omnipotent. God knows the past, the present, and all the possibilities of our future. Anticipation can be both delight and anguish. We experience the delight of anticipation when the purpose of God has come to pass. Here we experience joy and the fruits of our labors. It is the place where God's grace and favor rest upon us.

Another side of anticipation that many do not like can bring anguish and suffering. Anguish often represents pain. When anguish sets in, it is often uncomfortable, and we honestly don't like it. The Apostle Paul tells us,

"I reckon that the sufferings of this present time are not worthy to be compared with the glory which shall be revealed in us. For the earnest expectation of the creature waiteth for the manifestation of the sons of God" (Romans 8:18-19, KJV)

Short-term suffering will work in our favor in the long run. God knows our every need, even when we are suffering.

I know this from firsthand experience and from the suffering in my personal life, church ministry, marketplace, and parachurch ministry. My suffering represented the in-between season that I define as anticipation. God revealed His purpose to me in so many ways, but I had yet to see its manifestation. As mentioned earlier, heightened frustration caused me to move too quickly and more than often. Nevertheless, today, I recognize that my sufferings pushed me to another level in ministry, where I now experience the favor of God like never before. This was one of the first experiences where I realized the importance of being "in between" a blessing.

My life had taken a turn, and I learned some painful lessons. I needed a breakthrough; I needed God to speak to me. I needed answers, but I was not getting them. I repeatedly asked God why. I did not understand what God was doing, so I asked, "God, how can you reveal and unfold so much of my future to me, and then, I hear nothing?"

Things around me were falling apart even as God showed me that better was coming. I could not see it. I could not see images of how anything good could come from this period of suffering. When I reflected on my life during this period, I became keenly aware of my calling to a usual ministry in life.

At an early age, I knew that the things God was calling me

to, would not begin in a pulpit but in the streets. Yet I never saw an example and was often told I was too young and inexperienced. Out of so much rejection and fear, I found myself dumbing down my early vision and aspirations, dimming my dreams, and trying to fit in where God had not placed me. Again, let me mention my heightened frustration from never truly recognizing this place of being between anticipation and seeing the manifestation of God.

Personally, I was ready to give up and walk away, but one morning during prayer, I remember crying out to God and saying,

"Lord, how long must I wait? Will you forget me forever? How long will you turn your face away from me?" (Psalm 13:1:)

Looking at and witnessing how everything and everyone around me was flourishing, moving forward, and winning favor, I cried out to God, "What is going on?"

Yet, despite it all, I continued to remain faithful and steadfast. It was long and difficult. James 1:12 says, *"Blessed is the person who remains steadfast under trials, for when he stood the test he will receive the crown of life, which God has promised to those who love God"* (KJV).

Anticipation is about getting prepared for what God has shown us about what is to come.

Divine anticipation is a place where we know something is coming. Here, God invites and teaches believers to watch for God in action, often in the midst of chaos Divine anticipation is knowing that God is involved all the time and accepting the things we can't explain. Divine anticipation represents faith in motion.

While I did not know how or when, I knew that what was to come would be better than what had been. In the end, for me, it was all about trusting God and walking in faith. Becoming impatient will put us in a place where we attempt to control the conclusion instead of trusting God with the end results.

The attitude of anticipation for the manifestation of our promise involves trusting God with the next chapter of our life. Psalm 139:16 says, *"Your eyes saw my unformed body; all the days ordained for me were written in Your book before one of them came to be"* (NIV).

Think about the heroes of faith who anticipated the promises of God, knowing that what God promised would be fulfilled but never witnessing the real manifestation. Therefore, each had to trust and believe in The Lord. We often ask, "Can you trust God when you cannot trace Him?" Yes, you can. Remember that God is faithful to what He has promised. It was during this time of being in between the place of anticipation and seeing God's manifestation that I returned to school and completed my bachelor's degree, with an emphasis on the ministry.

During this time, I also had the opportunity to experience my first mission trip to Ghana, West Africa, where I connected with like-minded men and women who helped to shape my parachurch vision. Although this vision did not manifest itself for years, it clearly showed me that God indeed had a plan and purpose for my life, which would unfold according to God's timing, not mine.

Anticipation reveals God's plan for our lives, and it is contin-ually unfolding, happening minute by minute, day by day, and second by second. Consequently, my cries to God of "How long?" unfolded unbeknownst to me, and all I had to do was trust God, walk by faith and not by sight, and learn to wait.

In the 21st century, our issues with anticipation stem from the societal expectation for instant gratification. When such instant grati-fication does not happen, we become frustrated with God's timing and with ourselves. Spiritual frustration is the feeling of impatience and anxiety. I believe that any level of frustration can be difficult at times, leaving room for the enemy to dangle shining opportunities in front of you and causing many to get ahead of God's timing.

When you are in a state of anticipation and waiting for the manifestation of God's promises, be careful not to get ahead of God. Let's examine Scripture on getting ahead of God's timing. In Genesis 12:1-3, God promised Abraham that he would be the father of many nations. But Abraham was old, and time had passed. Sarah wanted to help God, and so she devised a plan to offer her maid Hagar to sleep with Abraham. Hagar and Abraham conceived a son and called him Ishmael. Sarah became angry and jealous because she had yet to conceive a child with Abraham.

The issue with society today is that we want what we want, when we want it; we want it right now, even when we are not ready for it. Learning to wait on God is a huge part of understanding God as we anticipate the unfolding of the promises given to us.

However, what do we do when we are in a place of anticipation, awaiting the full manifestation? According to Psalm 37:7 (KJV), *"Rest in the Lord and wait patiently for Him to act."* Turn it over to God. **Wait patiently, even when there is a delay.** God has not forgotten you, nor has He forgotten the promises He made to you. Remember, delay is not denial; it is just the place and holding pattern where God has you now. When you are in a place between anticipation and manifestation, Allow me to encourage you.

5 Simple Steps of How I Made It Over:
- Remember the promises of God for your life.
- Learn to wait on the Lord.
- Trust God through all of life's demands.
- Know that delay is not denial.
- Be reminded that God has not forgotten you.

Affirmations by Dr. Sanja Rickette Stinson

I will make it.

I Will Make It.

I am a Winner!

I will win and make it over.

God has a purpose and plan for me

BIOGRAPHY: *Dr. Sanja Rickette Stinson is an author, visionary entrepreneur, a nonprofit CEO. Her passion is to assist individuals in moving their vision from napkin to action, from action to reality, from reality to success, from success to purpose, and from purpose to creating a legacy for future generations. As a serial entrepreneur, author, Vision and Legacy Strategies/ Coach my passion is to provide in-person, one-on-one and digital training to individuals who are ready to awaken their dreams, activate their vision (s)* of becoming business owners and entrepreneurs creating a lasting legacy for generations to follow.

Dr. Sanja R. Stinson is the founding CEO/Executive Director of Matthew House, a daytime service center serving homeless men, women, and families in Chicago's Bronzeville area since 1991 a 501(c)3 charitable organization. Matthew House provides a wide variety of supportive services, including case management, skills assessment, job readiness training, two hot meals, shower services, healthcare, as well as permanent supportive housing.

I enjoy empowering women assisting them with birthing forth their vision, awakening their purpose that compels and creates a lasting legacy. I am the founder of Dr Sanja Coaching & Consulting Inc and Women on the Frontline International Fellowship and the Ruach Channel where she interviews women from around the world highlighting various entrepreneur conversations.

Dr. Stinson earned a bachelor's degree from DePaul University, a Master of Divinity from McCormick Theological Seminary, a Doctorate of Ministry from Northern Theological Seminary, and a Master of Education from Concordia University, an honorary Doctor of Ministry Degree from Ramah School of Theology.

11

The Soul Infection

By: Dr. TeKeisha Wade

The issue with society today is that we want what we want, when we want it; we want it right now, even when we are not ready for it. Learning to wait on God is a huge part of understanding God as we anticipate the unfolding of the promises given to us. Darkness is what I felt, until I got a full understanding of what I was experiencing, I felt lost. I had to go through the process to see the true meaning of darkness and to decide which path to take. I learned darkness was the opposite of light; because of this, I took it at face value.

Unconsciously, I started taking my own steps and my own routes of healing. I want to take you on the journey of traveling my own roads causing an unknown infection to spread.

One day, I made up my mind to leave my hometown and start a new life. I had grown tired of the toxicity around me and the moving in and out of an abusive relationship. So, I left, and

found myself homeless with my four children. Thank God, I was able to find a hotel to stay in

for a couple of weeks. Favor was really on us because the manager of the hotel allowed us to

reside there, in a suite, until I found housing. God blessed me with great co-workers. One of my co-workers referred me to her apartment manager, and he approved me for an apartment. I was so excited, and I immediately started to thank God. A month or so later, the kids and I moved into our new home.

Everything was going well for us. I even re-enrolled into college. But then I started to repeat my past. Even though I was miles away, I somehow moved back into an abusive relationship. The relationship was with my previous husband. We remarried, in my mind, his behavior would change, I was wrong, it did not. Somehow, I forgot he was a narcissist. After finding out about his multiple situation ships, I decided to file for another divorce. This left another wound to heal.

I thought putting him and the abuse in the back of my mind would cause the healing process to speed up. In my mind, I was healed and ready to find love again. I joined several dating sites including Facebook dating. I was excited to finally be in a healthy relationship. The more dates I went on, the more I started to bleed. Unconsciously, I was on a mission to find love.

I found myself going to the extreme. One day, I traveled three hours in a vehicle that needed brakes and new tires. I would leave in the middle of the night while my kids were asleep. I did not realize how much pain I was causing myself and my kids. Although I was joining myself with these individuals, I thought because I was going to church and praying, I would be just fine.

Guess what everyone, even though I had experienced the wrong ones, I ran into the right one. I was on cloud ten. I introduced him to the kids and my family. I even met his family. I just knew I had found my soulmate. I had never experienced this type of relationship. An individual that was so loving. He didn't just love me, but he loved my kids. We decided to take it to the next level by moving in together. After discussing future goals, we decided to move to Texas. This was the happiest I have ever been in a while. Things were coming together as planned. But there was something that I put in the back of mind as well, my marriage. I was still legally married.

What was I thinking? However, I had it all planned out. I was going to rush this divorce and soon afterwards, get married to my new guy. Unfortunately, it did not go the way I planned. I was lay-off from my job, my new guy broke off the relationship, and I had to move back home with my parents. I was devastated. I started to feel an overwhelming amount of anxiety that led to depression. I feared I would never get back on my feet. I decided to go on a journey of self-discovery. I had to get to the root of the problem. I went into worship, and I called out to GOD and JESUS. And yes, he answered. I did not know that a breaking, a pruning, came attached to the answer. When you pray, you must be prepared for the answer GOD is going to deliver. His delivery is not for the flesh, it is for the soul.

God truly started working on me. Again, I thought I can go through this process with just prayer and worship. A month or so after moving back home with my parents, I felt good enough to date again. I met this guy and we started spending a lot of time with each other. We met each other's family and even started attending church together. Two months into the relationship, he started to display abusive behaviors. The people around me; including his circle, tried to tell me to get out of the relationship. I decided to be stubborn and stay. The abuse got worse. I no longer could take the verbal, physical, and mental abuse. I decided to walk away from the relationship. Breaking away from that relationship opened a door that I was not ready to walk into.

I walked into a spiritual darkness. In this darkness, my mind, body and soul were exposed to an illness greater than any illness in the physical realm. It is not in the DSM-5 and not even in a medical dictionary. I went to several doctors including being rushed to the ER. I found a primary care doctor to examine me, and she said I looked like death. This prompted a nervous breakdown. She told me if I did not check myself into a mental facility, that she would call the authorities to force me. Even though I had decided to go before visiting her, her words frightened me.

I went back to the ER to be reevaluated and asked for mental health services. I was placed in this padded room that felt like prison. I started to hyperventilate and all I could think about was death. Upon evaluating me, I was admitted into a facility for 7-8 days. Within that time, the doctor was unable to diagnose me. He tried different types of medication; in which, none of them worked. He said he could not find anything wrong with me; however, he provided a general diagnosis. I was diagnosed with depression, anxiety, and a change/adjustment disorder. I was sent home with prescriptions. The medications prescribed were causing me to worsen mentally, emotionally, and physically. I felt so discouraged and confused. I went to four different mental health providers. To my amazement, one refused to provide care after speaking with me.

After this, I made another trip to another ER. I could not find an answer to the symptoms I was having. I went home and I cried so many tears. I called my friends and family to pray for me. I felt stuck in a place that I just knew I was not going to escape from. Then one day, after praying, the Holy Spirit answered. I was infected. It was a soul infection. I was experiencing an alarming amount of side effects. This was an awakening.

The infection was caused by living in spiritual darkness. Spiritual darkness is the state of an individual living apart from God. Little did I know, the sin from sleeping with guys that were not my husband causing them to be spiritual husbands while still being married and not having a healthy relationship with The Lord was causing me to experience a spiritual death.

I had to decide to surrender, die to self and do it God's way. I had to rebuild my relationship with Christ. I started following his instructions and let him walk ahead of me. Through the new journey, he has been my Physician. I am still standing and I am more aware of my purpose. God never left me during that process, and he will never leave you. I am here to tell you to never give up. Sometimes we must pause and focus. This also includes resetting. I encourage you to take as many resets needed. I want to leave you with a prayer that pushed me to my breakthrough.

God,

Grant me the Serenity to accept the things I cannot change, Courage to change the things I can and Wisdom to know the difference. Living one day at a time, accepting hardships as the pathway to peace, Taking, as He did, this sinful world as it is not as I would have it, Trusting that He will make all things right if I surrender to His will, That I may be reasonably happy in this life and supremely happy with Him forever in the next one.

In JESUS Name, Amen.

BIOGRAPHY: *Dr. TeKeisha Wade (Founder: Open Arms Connection LLC, Empower HIM Coaching, & Soul Care Xperience Academy), a Global Speaker, Certified Life Coach & Christian Counselor, #1 Best-Selling Author, & Founder/Editor-In-Chief of H.E. Magazine and S.H.E. Magazine. Her work is dedicated to empowering men and women to achieve their full potential and inspiring them to become advocates, change-makers, and leaders in their communities. In her practice, she is led by a vision of creating a high-quality coaching/counseling session that is relevant, thought-provoking, and rooted in inclusivity and diversity.*

Email Address: twade@openarmsconnection.com

12

God has Never Failed Me

By: Felica Golden Grimes

I can do all things through Christ who strengthens me. Philippians 4:13

My journey is not easy as it has its ups and downs. I know that feeling of helplessness as I suffered in silence with many health issues since I was born with congenital heart defect diagnosed with POTS (Postural Orthostatic Tachycardia Syndrome) and SVT (Supraventricular Tachycardia), to name a few medical issues. POTS is associated with many chronic illnesses that impact your daily life. It made me realize why I was so sickly, weak, falling, fainting as a child, even during my teenage years and adulthood.

I never really felt normal, so I appeared introverted from childhood to early adulthood. Looking back and even now, many things overstimulate me causing nervousness, migraines, heart palpitations, lightheadedness, etc. These effects still show when I am in large crowds of people. Loud noises, piercing sounds, thunderstorms, lawnmowers, and fireworks are utterly irritating, tremendously frustrating, and drive me crazy because I have become very noise sensitive. I only attended two concerts in my entire life because of the noise!

My chronic illnesses took a toll on my parents because I was always in and out of the cardiologist office or hospital. Although they never spoke about it, I am aware of how challenging it was for my parents because they would have to take off work. I suffered tremendously in silence for

most of my life. It was utterly unimaginable to learn all the heart surgeries were not successful and were misdiagnosed my entire life.

However, at age 35, I met a world specialist. My doctor considered me the most unique patient he ever diagnosed with POTS because of my physical abilities, yet highly functional with limitations. Essentially, my body adjusted over time and has some normalcy level with modifications to do everyday tasks. Therefore, no surgery nor medication can resolve my issues, but medication can control my symptoms. My heart diagnosis caused me to spiral into a silent depression for several years that I never got help for, that was a great mistake not to get appropriate help. Living in Texas and dealing with insane heat and crazy humidity literally flares my POTS condition. Imagine exercising without sweating, and if I sweat, it means, experiencing POTS flare-up. Yes, I've had some embarrassing moments leaving public events on a medical stretcher.

My husband has been my rock with all my ups and downs. He always reminds me to focus on what I can do and let the rest go, but it is not always easy to do so. Many times, I find myself comparing my life to others because many people travel to all kinds of exotic places, but my health limits me from experiencing some adventures. My sweet husband finds ways for me to still experience life by carefully planning our adventures and traveling during cooler months.

Most of the time, I am misunderstood by my friends and family because many never experienced how it feels to be chronically ill, and some days are better than others. Through the years, I learned to mask my illness by changing my appearance, so hairpieces and makeup became my new best friends. It made me become an expert chameleon to disguise discomfort or challenges. One area I excelled in is academics. I focused all my attention on acquiring a bachelor, three master's degrees, and currently pursuing a doctoral degree. Continuing my education has always been a haven for me and allowed me to feel accepted. One other area that I have genuinely embraced, and love is social media, for this gives me a lot of social outlets that I don't have in my personal life. Over several years, I have built online relationships, collaborations, partnerships, and streams of income.

My struggle taught me to live and adjust as needed. It also implies not being able to do what everyone else does; thus, many people think I am "flaky" whenever I decline an invitation or event. Consequently, I rarely get invites from people who know me and my condition. It's indeed a challenge to my social skills and competence; that's why I've learned to reinvent myself with that in my mind.

Interestingly enough, I have been underweight, normal size, and overweight for decades, so I totally can relate to all the ups and downs about weight and chronic pain. As a result of my heart diagnosis, I became an emotional eater for years because this was the easiest way to cope with my misery, personal issues, and stress due to compounding health challenges. I never honestly shared my inner thoughts or emotions. It was reflected in my increasing waistline and body parts. My health was slowly deteriorating because of my overweight issues. The more medications I was prescribed the more frustrated I became about my body image. Basically, I felt trapped in another body not looking like someone I clearly didn't recognize every day.

With a firm conviction to make myself better despite many

opposing views, I underwent LapBand surgery. However, without my knowledge, my first weight loss surgery failed severely! My lap band slipped and caused a lot of damage and significant scar tissue. It was enormously frustrating, and I felt like a failure for several years. Of course, people judged me all the time. So, my last resort was to undergo Bariatric Revision Surgery. Fast forward to 2016, and my life tremendously changed as I dared to get weight loss surgery. On Feb. 12, 2016, the surgery happened, and this started my new chapter in life.

However, I was affronted with another difficult decision: to move forward to get a gastric sleeve which implies another surgery. I had no idea that this would happen during surgery, such as a second hernia repair, major scar tissue, and a mysterious hole that had to be fixed, which extended my surgery three hours. So now I have a gastric sleeve (stomach is the size of a banana) in order to control my portion sizes. It was a life alternating surgery that ultimately led me to my weight loss journey.

Because I believed in myself every day that I would get better and lose weight, the process went smoothly. Initially, I had to lose 20 pounds in 3 weeks before surgery. That was challenging because if I didn't do it, I couldn't get the surgery. Proudly, I got it done! After surgery, every single day, I believed in myself and stayed committed to the process. I was determined to stop emotional eating and to improve my nutrition. As a result, I lost 140 pounds within a year. That's a total of 160 pounds I lost within 12 months! I was very laser-focused with an unstoppable attitude to achieve my goal. I admit it was one of the best decisions that I ever made.

I knew that after the gastric sleeve operation, the transformation would not only be physical but emotionally and mentally as well. Being assertive is my weapon. I had to fight back criticisms from other people and eventually learned to be braver than ever. I took pride in my decision and believed that I deserved this transformation. Therefore, I tried to live a healthy lifestyle and likewise availed different means and tools that could help me keep up with my maintenance –

getting back on track, losing weight, tightening skin, improving hair growth, and other related issues.

Bariatric surgery is way more challenging than anyone thinks. People call me a cheater because of my decision, but I did not let these criticisms affect me. They didn't pay for my surgery, nor all the protein, food, vitamins, prescriptions, and massive wardrobe so I simply ignored all the judgements and opinions. One thing is for sure, and I know it's nothing but the grace of God that got me this far in life from being overweight, depressed, now on track to maintain my health and weight.

My current lifestyle is about staying healthy and fit by gaining muscle tone, improving mobility, and flexibility. Honestly, there is no essential maintenance or accountability plan after bariatric surgery, and that's one main reason other people regain weight post-surgery. In my case, since my weight surgery, my health has tremendously improved along with my mobility. Although my chronic illness and pain are a part of my daily life, they have become more tolerable and manageable because of my healthy lifestyle choices. Yes, I eat crazy food sometimes, but I pay attention to portion control daily, increasing my protein, vegetable and fiber intake and consuming fewer carbohydrates. My heart is happy that I made myself first by keeping the weight off since my surgery. I still weigh myself, so when the holiday pounds or stress hits, I cut back. Making a conscious decision to cut back on my portions is one way to remember what worked at the beginning by resting my mindset to get back on track.

The journey is not easy, and the struggle is real! Despite this, I believe that God has brought me a mighty long way. I silently struggled with my weight issues for several years but overcame that challenging part of my life. This weight loss journey is a realization that nothing is unbearable with God by our side. I didn't lose faith. I trust the process and firmly believe that I can transform myself and my total lifestyle. The same applies to many aspects of life. Any person can be facing a difficulty like financial or health struggles. But only you and your faith and determination can lead you to achieve your goal. Being empowered to rise from any predicament or challenge is key to a successful life. I've helped many people get through the health and wellness journey by offering personal and group coaching. It's been indeed a wonderful experience making a positive impact on other people's mindsets and health goals.

Nevertheless, it is also important to always trust God's process. You may be wondering why you are given several health issues, that sometimes you feel overwhelmed and depressed. As a living testimony, God is only molding us in the way he wants us to be. Keep the faith that God will never fail you. The lessons in my life's journey are what keeps me going until now. Several years ago, I entered the world of health and wellness by helping my clients become laser-focused to achieve their personal health goals. I feel strong, fulfilled, and unstoppable with this commitment to changing people's lives through effective health and wellness management; I feel strong and fulfilled.

I pray this serves as a testimony to support your friends and family facing health issues, emotional and mental stress during life's challenging moments. This is something that I wanted to share with you. To show my support and say "You are loved and appreciated" all the time. God listens, and He will take care of you. We are one in this journey, so let us help each other out in the best way possible.

BIOGRAPHY: *Felicia Golden Grimes is a Money Detective, Financial Educator, Health and Wellness Coach. Her goal is to transform your life and help you find money you can't find. She has led hundreds of people over the last 10 years teaching about financial freedom, money, relationships, confidence, passion, and purpose so people can obtain abundance. Felicia has over 28 years of extensive teaching, primarily working within the collegiate environment at community college and university levels. She has a diverse skill set within higher education as a corporate business developer, workforce director and manager, faculty member, faculty coordinator, department chair, recruiter, educational consultant, curriculum developer, and online trainer.*

EDUCATION & AWARDS *Her portfolio likewise reflects diverse*

educational background including Bachelor of Arts in English, Master of Reading Education, Master of Education in Curriculum Technology, Master of General Psychology, currently in progress to obtain Doctor of Business Administration degree. Felicia is a recipient of the National Institute for Staff and Organizational Development (NISOD) Teaching Excellence Award, Tarrant County College Chancellor's Award for Exemplary Teaching Nominee and received various student development achievement awards.
https://www.feliciagrimes.com/

13

From Hurt to Healing

Gloria Walton

"We may encounter many defeats, but we must not be defeated." Maya Angelo

Epidurals, muscle relaxers and a walking cane held me hostage for three years. I was injured during an emergency investigation. A mother was threatening to kill her child. As the intake investigator It was my job to assess risk and protect this child from his abusive parent. I had no idea the severity of my injuries until trying to walk became so painful that laying down was all I could do. I loved my job as a child protection service investigator and second job as a SPRU Worker (special protective response unit) an after-hour investigator. There was little or no protection when I found myself amid an enraged psychotic parent.

Being a field investigator and determined to protect children, placed me on the front line where I was always vulnerable to physical and verbal attacks. Susceptible to danger, seen and unseen. I spent the next three years in and out of hospitals. There goes my opportunity to transfer to the sexual assault victim's agency. That was going to be my next career move. Instead, I'm collecting workers compensation, raising three children, two mortgages, and a declining lifestyle in which I had grown accustomed to. I owned a single-family home within three miles of my employment. To give my children a better educational experience, I moved to Sussex County 46.8 miles away and the only African American family in our neighborhood. Unfortunately, my mother and greatest supporter died two years prior to my accident. She had custody of my niece and newborn nephew, who was transferred to me. My father lived in a rehabilitation facility in Connecticut. His cancer was in remission, so he moved into my single-family home to help care for his only grandson. When friends asked me about my health, my response was always "pain never killed anyone" but oh...how that is not the truth. Every day the severity of back pain from herniated discs, sciatic nerve and neck pain made me think death was an option. But who would care for my children? I did the mind over matter, read my bible, and followed doctor's orders.

Pills, epidurals, diagnostic test after test and no lasting relief, I was in the battle of my life, physically, emotionally, and spiritually. After the first year and only 70 percent of my salary, I still had hope of returning to both jobs. The doctors representing my employer recommended back surgery with a warning. I would probably lose a large percentage of my mobility. I already had limited mobility, shuffling my feet to walk with a cane. Could surgery be worse than what I had? Hurting, crying, and emotionally drained I sought the Lord, but there was no miraculous healing. Instead, there became another layer of pain. My worker's compensation was discontinued because I missed several physical therapy appointments. I could no longer drive the distance. Some days I was so disoriented I could only sleep. One day after my children left for school, I decided to cook dinner early. I put the pots on and totally forgot about them. I slept through a kitchen fire and a house of smoke. During my next doctor's visit, I described the feelings of being disoriented and unable to wake up. Well, it turned out that my level of medication was too strong.

Unfortunately, when the medication level was lowered, I still experienced mental fogginess, fatigue, and physical pain. To have my compensation reinstated I had to keep my appointment with the Workers Compensation's Orthopedic Surgeon. Driving from Sussex County to Union County was a familiar ride. In fact, I had been a SPRU worker for both counties. The next incident could have ended my life. I remember driving down route 80 East. There I was in a parking lot and no memory of how I got there. Disoriented, I didn't recognize any of my surroundings.

As I staggered out of my car, God used a stranger to ask if I was ok. This was divine intervention. He stopped a police car and stood there until the police officer reached me before he disappeared. I still wonder about that moment. The police didn't call an ambulance. He asked me questions and left. I sat in my car for a few hours before I proceeded back home because I had already missed my workers compensation doctor's appointment. The same night I was taken to the hospital and discharged. I was driven to a friend's home, so sick I could only lay on the floor. The following morning, risk management granted permission for my hospital visit. The ER doctor said I needed a spinal tap and without hesitation I signed. Shocked at the results I was hospitalized for seizures. The doctor explained all the disorientation I had experienced was in fact a seizure. Upon admission for eight days, I was treated with three different seizure medications. I refused phenobarbital because all my clients with a seizure disorder took phenobarbital. I saw the effects firsthand. I settled with Tegretol.

Unfortunately, within three months I was back in the hospital, body at the highest-level of pain, borderline depressed and questioning God about my healing. I was sick and tired of being in pain, hospitals, and doctors. I wanted my life back! Although I had maintained a prayer life, my prayers were now more targeted. I had experienced God in a different way. Driving with undiagnosed seizures, I could have been dead. I knew that God alone had sustained me during my time of weakness and pain. How did I make it over all the pain and disappointment? First My conversation with God and myself changed. I stopped trying to negotiate with God. During my times of disorientation, I couldn't remember the scriptures, but now I was clear on what the word of God said about me. No more God please heal me. My self-talk changed to a position of healing. I have not had a seizure in thirty years, returned to work for ten years and took an early retirement.

BIOGRAPHY: Gloria Walton is an author, advisor, humanitarian, and almoner, with an inherent gift to aid in the healing of those burned by diverse traumas. Gloria has determined that it is her life's calling to serve and heal those, carrying burdens of oppression and abuse, through her unique skills acquisition including a blending of management theories, a command of social service's practice and procedures, and a deeply ingrained spiritual commitment, coupled with her interpersonal insight, and a genuine heart for people. CEO/Founder of Most Excellent Way Life Center, and Urban Behavioral Health Services Inc. Host of Mothers & Daughters Candid Conversations and Something of Substance & Conference Host: Collaborating Women's International Conference.

Survival of a Chosen One

By: Reverend Jacqueline Lulu Brown

"He who is not courageous enough to take risks will accomplish nothing in life." - Muhammad Ali

"Ye have not chosen me, but I have chosen you, and ordained you, that ye should go and bring forth fruit, and that your fruit should remain: that whatsoever ye shall ask of the Father in my name, he may give it you." John 15:16

After Jesus stated how much he loved his disciples and that

they had not chosen Jesus, rather, he chose them (John 15:13-16), he faithfully acquainted them with the world's hatred of them, and what they must expect. His words do not imply any doubt about it, "if the world hate you"; spoken as if they had some experience of it already, and might look for more, when their master was gone from them. To engage their patience under it, he says, "ye know that it hated me before it hated you." There is a survival kit required for those who are chosen.

I am familiar with people who hate or dislike me. Moreover, I've experienced someone's disdain based on my race, that I'm operating in my genius, showing up in excellence with compassion, integrity, divine love, and most importantly operating in the Holy Spirit. I made the decision early on in my Corporate Technology career that I would not compromise myself for gain. I was never going to become a corporate clone and certainly would never become part of the "good old boys". I stood in my God given gifts and dared to be different. I taught others to do the same and it was by these basic principles that I became an excellent Leader. I knew that I was chosen.

My parents gave me two names, Jacqueline, and Lulu, but I'm fondly known as "Lulu." I was named Lulu after the endearing and mischievous cartoon character, Little Lulu. The character Lulu and I had a lot in common; we were resourceful, resilient little girls who are very smart. The Lulu in me was viewed as "a piece of work," however.

I rarely initiate a battle unless provoked but I do have an appetite to fight for justice and equality. This started at a young age thanks to my oldest Sister, Denise. I was eccentric, referred to as a "busy body", imaginative, and that I talked far too much. Mischief and trouble were never my goal but often the case. Over the years I've learned to love and cherish my unique qualities and "crazy" imagination because therein is my genius. God gives us marvelous talents and gifts. It took years for me to appreciate my uniqueness and the power that resides within.

I always knew in the deepest part of my heart that I was destined for greatness, however; I never spoke the words out aloud and I certainly didn't envision that I'd carry a message to the masses of Women that is often unpopular, yet necessary for growth and the ability for one to reach their highest elevation. More importantly, I didn't know that such a calling and being "chosen" would come with a major transformation and healing taking place in my life. My divine calling meant a willingness to hear the truth and go through my own process of awakening, self-discovery, reclaiming my self-worth, self-forgiveness, identifying my genius, operating in my authentic self, and allowing God to order my footsteps.

By the time I was in my adolescent years I was consistently living in what I later learned to be "fight-or-flight", a physiological reaction in response to stress. There were many traumatic experiences taking place in my family that kept me in the familiar fight-or-flight response for years to come as I normalized dysfunction. Domestic abuse between my parents resulted in my mother's fall from a 2nd story window. She survived but required a major brain operation and suffered other critical injuries. I witnessed family members suffering from drug addiction, alcoholism, and mental illness up close and personal. There was the absence of one or both parents during key adolescent periods which brought feelings of abandonment. My Dad was the more consistent figure in my life, however.

In contrast to the negative exposures and traumatic experiences, I was being raised by my wonderful great-aunt and her Husband. I was given to them at about 3 months old. This was my grandmother's sister. My Father's side of the family were the "Cosby Show" only it was the turbulent 60's and they didn't have "the cash". Everyone in my dad's generation were educated, worked good jobs, and lived in nice homes. My grandmother's generation were classy, smart, and worked hard to provide the best they could for their family.

My Father's Mother and my aunts took us to church consistently. I knew there was a God, understood how to pray, was baptized when I was 8 years old and was on the Jr. usher board at church. However, I would not experience God in the form of a personal relationship with enlightenment until my late teenage years; my first Husband was a Pentecostal Pastor's son.

I met my first Husband as a teenager in high school. His Mother was immediately drawn to me. My first Husband was an only child and his mother, a great Woman of faith and wisdom, always wanted a daughter. I became her daughter, and our relationship was that of Naomi and Ruth until she departed this life. My first Husband's Mother and Father drew my mother to Christ with divine love. My Mother became a great Woman of God in the Ministry. The insanity of my parents' relationship dissolved. My Mother and Father became friends with a peace between them that surpassed everyone's understanding. My mother's prayers, faith, and deep relationship with God had her give the proclamation that God was going to save her daughters. This was manifested not many years after she spoke it. We became Evangelists, Missionaries, and Elders. My Mother is now 93 years old, and she remains active in the Ministry.

The blessings of God didn't come without pain and heartache. When you are chosen by God, the enemy comes to kill, steal, and destroy. I went through turbulent times with my first Husband. He was addicted to drugs and alcohol. I suffered greatly while married to him. I had 3 small children and there seemed to be no light at the end of my tunnel. I was immature in my relationship with God. The enemy set a trap and I fell into it. My first Husband and I parted. I was broken, bruised, and ripe for the enemy. I became involved in an abusive relationship and almost lost my life twice; yet again, there was that fight-or-flight on a consistent basis. This time it was fight-or-die.

There came a night that I decided to "fight and live". I'd had enough and either I would perish repenting or God would bring me out of the bondage I'd become so entangled in. God told the enemy "She shall live and not die."

As the years went by, I grew in ministry; I enjoyed being used by God and I loved doing anything that involved women's empowerment. The enemy was persistent on my trail, and I often made mistakes but this time I persevered. I studied and received wisdom, knowledge, and a better understanding of the Proverbs 31 woman.

The years went on and the trials and tests grew stronger, but I continued to take the lessons learned and move forward in my purpose. In 2010 there was a strong shift beginning to happen in me. There was a heightened awareness in my spirit driving me to go higher, deeper, and seek God's divine purpose for my life on a whole new level. By 2011 I'd received a deeper understanding of the things God downloaded in my spirit.

I was a high-flying corporate Leader with tremendous success in my career of Information Technology and Engineering. Yet, I always knew that cooperate success was not my life's "true" calling and that there was more divine purpose to be discovered. At this time my God's purpose was burning inside of me like "fire shut up in my bones." In 2014 I began reaching out for guidance and help across all areas of my life, spiritually, intellectually, and mentally. My outcomes were self-discovery, reclaiming my self-worth, self-forgiveness, identifying my brilliance and genius, and bringing into alignment my spirit and authentic self.

This was the inner work required before I could move on further.

Too often we are attempting to impart onto others something we don't have ourselves. God's revelation showed me the need to transform the lives of professional women and help them come from living "behind the mask", a mask that I knew all too well and had broken through. I saw and accepted the assignment to revolutionize our Black Churches by designing programs that address the unique needs of Women from a God centered perspective of freedom and not the current chains that enslave us under the disguise of Godliness.

Many people are not walking in their God given superpowers. Who they are authentically is not in divine alignment with their spirit. As people of God, we speak clichés about "the sky's the limit" when God has given us power, authority, and dominion over all things. **"There is no sky and there are no limits except the ones' that we create** for ourselves." We need a radical approach to addressing the needs of women seeking their purpose. Many are called but few are chosen. We must lead and minister with new insights about our feminine power, our divine gifts, and how to make radical positive change in the lives of others. I am a "CHOSEN SURVIVOR" and I know that every woman deserves a bright shining life that sings to their soul.

MY AFFIRMATION

"I am victorious over every demonic hindrance, sickness, disease, dis-ease, and lack or want are not my portion, I shall revolt against anything that tries to interrupt my destiny. No weapon formed against me shall prosper, I am prosperous, I am whole, I am enough, I am brilliant, I am genius." JLB

MY SUPPLICATION

God, I thank you in the name of Jesus for giving me the courage to answer your calling and accept your divine purpose for my life. I submit myself and acknowledge God in all my ways asking that my path is divinely directed. As I go into prayer, I pray that God, you will manifest your presence in my life. I humble myself before you God. Thank you, God, because the weapons of my warfare are not carnal but are mighty to the pulling down of satanic strongholds. I pray that God will release legions of warrior angels to assist me in this battle. Let God's angelic host bind and restrain every demonic resistance. Let them destroy every satanic opposition. God, I pray that you will dispatch special angels of battle to evacuate stubborn spirits and their agents to the land of the wicked for mass destruction by divine power. I put on the whole armor of God that I may withstand the wiles of the enemy. In the name of Jesus, I've chosen to take a stand against doubt, fear, and be strong and courageous as God, you've chosen me. I declare and decree that today, the angels of favor are released to favor me, and the angels of prosperity are dispatched to bring prosperity and abundance to me in the name of Jesus. I praise you God and of er up this prayer. Amen.

BIOGRAPHY: *Jacqueline Lulu Brown, fondly known as "Lulu" is a*

dynamic woman who spent 40+ years in the Information Technology and Engineering arena. During that time, she held technical, management, and executive leadership roles throughout the world.

One of the things that "Lulu" discovered during her career and travels was that women in their career, business, and ministry, were feeling the heavy burden of silently carrying their "unsaid." These unsaid challenges are often not openly discussed because of secret shame, and ultimately, the fear of revealing one's true self. In 2010, "Lulu's" true calling and genius was burning like "fire shut up in her bones." Additionally, Lulu received a deep calling to revolutionize today's church with a unique message for the masses of Women.

Now, as a Transformational Speaker, Elevation Leader, Women's Empowerment Consultant, Mentor, and Licensed Minister/Elder, she's spoken, coached, and mentored Women and Young Girls across the world, including India, the United Kingdom, Australia, Israel, Spain, Antigua, Mexico, and Aruba. Lulu's purpose and focus with her business, Revolution Ascension LLC, is to provide a safe sacred space for open, honest, and raw conversation. She and her team bring a comfortable, yet a radical way of helping women see their greatness and brilliance in the middle of their challenges. The key outcomes for clients are alignment with spirit and authenticity and unleashing one's Divine Feminine Power.

Lulu values innovation, diversity, service, individuality, and equality. She believes every woman deserves a bright shining life that sings to their soul.

Lulu holds a Bachelor of Science degree, several Technical, Executive Leadership, and Coaching Certifications, including the ICF (International Coaching Federation); she is a "Women of Color in Technology" Award recipient and is listed in "Worldwide Who's Who" for excellence in Information Technology. Lulu hosts a weekly segment, "Be Real Be Raw Be You with Lulu - The Lulu Experience" on iWorship96, an international radio station and is also on the Black House Media channel streaming on the XOD platform. She is a co-author of the books "31 Ways of Influence", "Audacity to Shine", and I am a Black Woman the Next Level", of which, she is the International Ambassador. Additionally, Lulu is the VP of Operations for BHC Media. Naturally philanthropic, "Lulu" also serves on the board of "The Way-Out

Ministries INC" a 501c3 corporation, as their Chairperson and Chief Program Of icer (CPO). She is married to Kevin Alan Brown with a blended family of six adult children, seventeen grandchildren, and three great-grandchildren.

15

How Far I Have Come

Jeanine Bunzigiye

This story is about Jeanine's journey from sadness and rejection to living authentically and operating from abundance. We all have moments. Life comes with its own challenges and put us in positions where we feel like we are stuck, or we are going in circles. I do recall 6 years ago was a year when my life was very hard for me. I lost my sister and my brother back-to-back, 3 months apart from each other. That situation was very hard for me and my family. Sometimes I asked myself if I prayed enough for them and why God did allow that to happen in my family. It was very hard emotionally. I see how my nephews and nieces are alone now, and as a family I had to step in as an Aunty and be there for my sister and my brother's children. Even though I was still questioning God why all of this happened, and I knew that I needed to seek God on another level, it was really the most intense time in life. I was able to focus on my relationship with God on another level. Because not only I knew that I couldn't make it without God, but I knew that he was my only source for everything. I needed another dose of strength to be able to be there for my family as well.

Often, I read the book of Job in the bible, because it helps me a lot. *I started making a habit of really spending time in worship, praise and telling God no matter what, I will still believe him and only depend on him alone.* I started feeling confident that God is there with me in my pain, and I started showing up daily by talking to my family and my close friends. Remember, Job focused on God and didn't give up no matter what. This was the beginning of my healing. It was a process and I started taking one day at
the time. There were days where I felt like just staying in my room, and I don't feel like talking to anyone. Even in that moment I was still praising God, because it was a commitment to myself that no matter what I will give him the best worship. Because God is my peace, and He is my strength in it all. Even though it wasn't what I was feeling, I was committed to being consistent in my praise and worship. The book of my job was really my inspiration every time I was feeling alone or depressed.

I went before God and told him everything I was feeling or experienced, like how my family and I felt alone, because the place that my big sister had in my family was important. Since she transitioned, we still feel her absence big time. I was telling God to help us daily to fill that gap because my sister and brother played big roles in my family. There were projects that my sister and I started that for months I couldn't focus on. After being in his presence daily, I did find the courage to face them. Today, I am happy to say that I did continue to focus on those projects. I am in a place where I feel like it was meant for me to continue her legacy and one day, she will see all the projects come to fruition. I am encouraging everyone to look up to God and to really express yourself. Tell God how you feel. If you feel alone or empty, tell Him. Because at the end of the day, the only place I felt refuge and comfort was in His presence.

God is the only one who never gets tired of you. For 24 hours, He is always available to get you through no matter what.

Create a routine that you can stick with daily. Don't go by what you feel because your emotions can trick you big time. Truly worship God no matter what! Let us depend on His strength and that is how we will overcome. Know that whatever you are going through will be a testimony for many who will need to hear it one day. Sometimes our challenges are tests that we must pass. If you don't pass or learn from it, it will repeat itself and you will find yourself in the first situation because you didn't really learn how to surrender yourself to him daily. Do this so you can refresh and receive new strength from God.

Many people today are always asking me where you get your energy from. They think that I don't go through anything because I always present myself as a happy person. To me, life is all about how you manage the situation and not what really happens when you do come across the situation. Sometimes we only share the results with people, not the process and not necessarily what you experience. You do share with people what you learned as lessons and what can help someone as well. Challenges come every day, and they will continue to come but the most important things are how you chose to manage them daily.

Because if you allow situations to consume you, it will take over and you will miss your lessons. Then, fear will take over most of your time and your journey will be more complicated. I encourage you to decide to face problems together with God, get the support you need from others and spend time with God daily. Let us make sure He is our only source for everything. Let God be in the driver seat in every situation. It won't be easy but when you give him the driver seat and you depend on his direction, he will direct your path as the bible says. Today I am proud to say that I have learned my lesson. I yield the driver seat in my life to God. He does direct my path and my healing continues. Now, I encourage friends, family, and you to do the same because He does direct our paths. And it is much easier to be directed by him than trying to figure things out on our own.

SOCIAL: https://www.youtube.com/c/EmpoweringYouTV

16

My Warpaint and Ribbons Journey

Karen Van Buren

"Beauty is an attitude.. there's no secret." Estee Lauder

"Beauty begins the moment you decide to be yourself." Coco Chanel

Lying in bed my head would not stay still. All I wanted to do was rest, but my head literally was moving by itself. I laid there in disbelief that this was my new reality. Doctors in the neurology department said this was permanent and I would deal with this condition for the rest of my life. The rest of my life? Well, I was practically given a timeline of my life expectancy when diagnosed with my cancer. They gave me two years... They said five years if I was lucky. Now I had to grasp the concept of fighting for my life while enduring these painful spasms!

These spasms were a result of the cancer treatment. I found out eventually it was drug induced from the anti-nausea medication used during my chemotherapy treatments. Until I found out exactly what it was doctors speculated the cancer was moving to my brain. Trying not to be fearful of this prognosis I prayed an awful lot. It is a very sobering thought to know you're dying. An unnerving feeling when you have just reached your thirties. I was a single Mom, 32, bought my first home and was in the process of starting a business when I was diagnosed with cancer. I was in a relationship I was very happy in. He treated me like a queen, but I expressed that I thought we should take a break from one another while I addressed my health. I still remember him saying, "You can't make that decision for me. I want to be there for you. My grandmother faced breast cancer and I was there for her. I will be there for you, too."

He was there for me. He was very supportive. I remember getting so sick during chemotherapy treatment that I was lying on his bathroom floor late at night and could barely move to get myself to the toilet to get sick. He'd hold me up while I would throw up until I reached the point of dry heaving. I am thankful as I reflect on the help he gave me during such a brutal time in my life. He was at my bedside with my father as I was wheeled out to the recovery room after surgery. With tubes hanging out of my chest while feeling excruciating pain, I was relieved to see both their faces as I woke up from the anesthesia. He played in the NFL for years. My diagnosis came in June so he could not be there for me through each and everything. He had to go to training camp, and he was now playing for another team in another city. Or so I thought...

Turns out that was not the case. As I was facing my own mortality, keeping my household going and raising a little 8-year-old boy by myself I learned that my serious boyfriend had been lying to me. That particular year he was not picked up to play in the NFL. I'm sure he was dealing with his own feelings because of that but lying to me was absolutely unnecessary. I wasn't dating him because he was in the NFL. I'm not sure why he lied. I found out he was dating another girl behind my back as well. It's one thing to be a cheater or a womanizer but exercising those traits to your significant other while they're battling for their life is an extremely selfish act. I spoke to the woman he was cheating with. She said she knew who I was. She admitted she knew about me. She told me that he cheated on his wife with her and why would I expect to be any different. She told me she wasn't going anywhere so I should just accept it. That was something I was never going to accept. I had already suggested him going to live his life while I addressed my treatment, but he said he wanted to be there for me. This scenario was not an example of that. It would ultimately cause me more stress. I felt betrayed.

To add insult to injury I found a cassette tape in his VCR that wasn't what I expected. Turns out he had been hiding a camera in his house and taping himself with other women. As the video came on a date/time came across the TV and it read the exact day I was getting my first chemotherapy treatment. He literally was with a woman as I was being stuck with a painful needle in my hand to administer my chemo agents. I sat in the chair for hours receiving my treatment. He told me he was with his team that day. I'll never understand the motivation behind a cheater's mentality, but it's literally the lowest form of a person having little to no self-respect or self- discipline for themselves. Someone who cheats typically is good at lying because falsehood has become their narrative. I was hurt by this clear indication of having no regard for my feelings. I feel like the girl participating was also at fault for wanting to keep it going even when she knew of me. I decided to end the relationship because I knew I did not deserve such treatment.

He begged me not to and said it would not happen again, but at that point battling my cancer and fighting for my life took more priority over any relationship.

I believe in the GOLDEN RULE: Do unto others as you want done unto you (Matthew 7:12) is how the Bible quotes it. In other words, "Treat others the way YOU want to be treated." It's not that hard. To think HOW I MADE IT OVER the betrayal at that time was placing my focus on something else. I placed my focus on my health. HOW I MADE IT OVER my health trials was merely to continue treatments and concentrate on my healing. I never concentrated on me dying during my cancer journey. HOW I MADE IT OVER my spasms is a tough one to talk about. My head moved to the point where it looked like a fish out of water at times. I looked like I had a bobble head on my shoulders. It was very humbling. My spasms got so violent that my chin locked on my right shoulder and kept me locked for almost 4 years. I looked very contorted, one side of my neck was huge, with my muscles stuck in a hypertrophy state. My other muscles responded around it, forming a lump on the top of my back. My spasms moved to my legs and contorted them to the point where I could not walk at all. I was placed in a wheelchair each time that happened. HOW I MADE IT OVER my spasms was fervent prayer. I prayed through each of my trials I mentioned above, but my spasms actually made me feel like I was fighting real life demons.

When you come up against demons you better be prepared for the spiritual warfare that comes along with that battle. My "Warpaint and Ribbons" battle is how I label it. Being an esthetician with a concentration in the cosmetic industry as a traveled makeup artist, "war paint" has been my specialty. Going through the start of colon cancer, piggy backed by breast cancer only to be riddled with spasms from a brain injury put me in the societal norm of claiming a colored ribbon that stood for each nonprofit cause I was fighting. I had overcome a domestic violence relationship earlier in my twenties which gave me another ribbon to claim. As I fought each battle, I spiritually put my war paint on like a warrior would as I battled each fight.

I reunited with a man I was engaged to three years prior during my medical trials. He was there as a friend and a support system for my son who was 8 years old at the time. We married within the next year but had put it off due to medical insurance. Medical insurance is such a racket for the person going through all the medical issues. We got pregnant during my chemotherapy after doctors told me I was going infertile. We were encouraged to abort the baby. There were all kinds of medical reasons why. We were told I would more than likely lose the baby because I conceived during chemo. It is safe to administer chemotherapy in the second and third trimester, but not the first. We were told being pregnant raised my hormones and my hormones were feeding my breast cancer. We were told if I was able to carry and deliver the baby that to prepare ourselves for a child with major malformations. HOW I MADE IT OVER again was prayer. My prayers were concentrated so much on my healthy baby being born. My prayers came true! **As I write this my healthy baby boy is a normal (PRAISE GOD) and a very handsome 17-year-old.** His father and I share custody now. I am remarried and 18 years out from my cancer. I do still experience spasms now, but I push myself as I always have. I still have trials in life that come and go as all of us do, but this HOW I MADE IT OVER book project is a reminder to all of us that we are meant to share our stories. This is just part of mine. I pray that God touches whoever reads our stories.

SOCIAL: Warpaint and Ribbons https://www.facebook.com/livingoutloud4life

17

The Lotus Blossom

Lanashane Robert

Be still and know I am God

It was a morning like no other I had experienced before.

As I laid in bed motionless, my thoughts spun in loops. Desperate to ascertain precisely, how I had arrived at this point.

Over a short space of time my heart had become laden with unfathomable sadness.

My eyes which had grown dull, anxiously searched the empty space for answers. Like every other time, their search was futile – I felt anesthetized. A heart that once sang out melodies of joy was brusquely silenced.

In the most unexpected turn of events, I was dragged into the nightfall of despair. Shadows that tormented my mind even though scattered, had slashed me into hopelessness. Sadness and misery coerced their way into my life. Incessantly re-living the heart wrenching day when I hunched over a semi warm body. In a trance-like state I met my fatal realization... my mom was no longer with me. The 21$^{st \, of}$ April 2017, a dreadful day which will forever be etched in my memory...all I had known and loved for 46 years had taken flight. At one fell swoop I'd lost my mother, my best friend, my confidante, my pillar of strength and soulmate all at once.

Many heightened barriers closed in to keep me prisoner in the days that followed. Emotions and hurt collided with deep seated fear. In the zenith of darkness demons were let loose, decreed to taunt me into desolation. Spanning over a few weeks, and as life events stacked up against me, I found myself becoming emotionally, mentally, and eventually physically feeble.

Yet in all the chaos I heard the softest whisper that was stirring something in me - to shake the anguish out of me.

The soft caring voice and caresses of a gentle nudge, which I knew all too well formed a band of light around my heart. It started out with a tenor of affection I'd become to depend on. Whispers of love from my mom.

In a moment of silence, I heard the sweet voice of her soul. Each word that followed held the promise of hope and of belief.

Much to my surprise the whisper found its crescendo in the stillness, as the words of Khalil Gibran rang out.

"When you are sorrowful, look again in your heart, and you shall see that in truth you are weeping for that which has been your delight.

Some of you say Joy is greater than sorrow and others say,
"Nay sorrow is greater" but I say unto you, that they are inseparable.
Together they come, and when one sits alone with you at your bode;
remember that the other is asleep upon your bed. "

The words lingered on long after, and against the backdrop of autumn something very peculiar revealed itself in my life. It was difficult to imagine only a few weeks ago the same trees danced to glory of summer days. Once more, a season arrived upon them that rendered them helpless. As the grip of colder days set in, the trees reluctantly let go of their leaves. Towering giants gloomily watched as each of their leaves were ripped off their branches only to meet their end. Lifeless each leaf tumbled through unfounded space.

Autumn is a beautiful season, yet everything seems to wither away.

No matter what the seasons cast their way, trees had found a means to survive and to be beautiful at the same time.

I on the other hand, felt incapable to handle what life was now hurling my way. Even though once strong, I was not flexible. It would seem that I had just become dry and brittle to a point of lifelessness.

That is when everything in me seemed to collapse as I felt dwarfed by giants. Whilst encircled by rumbling sounds of defeat, bringing me to my knees. Wisdom which once fashioned my life was sucked out of me, and in its place fear and terror hastily set up camp. And in the hands of grief, I had forgotten my anchors of life - leaving me feeling crippled with dismay and blinded by darkness.

Grief and adversity seldom knock on Life's door - rather it creeps through cracks and crevices sedately it spins a web around its target.

And so, it was for me. With each passing day the darkness's embrace grew stronger.

Riddled with fear and gridlocked by terror, I'd consigned to oblivion my reserve of strength and anchors of faith. Grief had wormed its way and delighted in making me feel miniscule. Framing me with a false conviction of being abandoned and alone.

I dismissed from mind traces of hope in my present moment, therefore I had to rewind to my past. I had to call up my mind's mirror to see the reflections of her mother's love. Amidst those reflections I would see the strong brave woman she was. I would find faith and love waiting to guide me to places of joy. I was the same woman, only due to current context was like a rose buried under the weight of the cruel winter snow.

I had to slowly climb out from my downward spiral of depression and darkness. In a flash from the past, I recalled the life my mom wanted for me. I dwelled upon the hurt, pain and anguish; she'd overcome in her own troubled life to become the lotus rising from muddy waters. My melancholia state would never be the legacy she would leave behind. Inspired by memories of her tenacity, love and recalled words of encouragement, I too mustered resilience to rise.

My action was fueled by the words of Jack Thorne - "*Those we love never truly leave us – there are things death cannot touch*". I made a conscious decision to stop whispering words of discouragement and trepidation and began to pick up the pieces of my life. Before long I assembled the courage to pierce that which had ringfenced my aspiration.

Only once seated with darkness, does the light become appealing. Sometimes it takes the pain to find the will for change. Little by little I learnt through a powerful soul connection with my mother, to nurture my wounds and to feed my self-confidence.

With time I acknowledged that courage is never born without fear. Fear is the quintessence on which courage is refined. Only upon reflection on the past that everything was pieced together. **There's purpose in pain and there's meaning in madness. There's triumph in truth, but not if you don't learn from the roles they play in your story. It's time to call yourself out on your excuses**!

With an empowered thought and by guiding grace I stepped slowly away from the edge of grief onto a path of radical accountability for my future actions. Discomfort leads to growth, and it was these conscious actions that lay the foundation of deep and authentic resilience. Moments, we embrace reverence of all which occurred in our lives, becomes a pivotal moment that set our souls alight. Emerging out of grief being both soft and strong, is a combination very few can master.

That was my tipping point, which unleashed the power to change anything in my life.

With steely determination, intended focus to step into the light - something astonishing inspirited my attention. In a spirit of enquiry, I became acquainted with wisdom, which camouflaged wounds are seeds of exponential favour patiently waiting to blossom into fragrant flowers.

When you silently decide to step aside from the chaos, you begin a journey at your own pace in your own lane. It's precisely the time when all that was once hidden from you, starts to show up for you. Gracefully empowering you to claim being a victor over a victim mentality... if only for you to fly close to the sun. Whilst allowing you to relish in the promise that change is deserving and a beautiful rejuvenation from inside out.

The foundation on which BelleLana Collection was born to honour my mom's legacy. The hand-embroidered fashion-art jewelry range has earned me the title of South African Fashion Week Designer, a title I had never sought. My pieces are showcased across the globe, and I have received invites to participate at Milan, Paris and San Francisco Fashion Weeks.

A love between a mother and child knows no bounds and through my creations we share a beautiful space between Heaven and Earth.

Never doubt the power of love, faith and hope fueled by action – it moves mountains!!!

BIOGRAPHY: After years as a communication specialist and senior manager in telecoms. Lanashane ventured into establishing self-owned businesses, her flourishing potential has awarded her the title of designer and artist of her jewelry brand. Lanashane's creations have featured at international art exhibitions, and she has been invited to participate in international fashion weeks. Her determination and passion to inspire and motivate people has paved the way for her novel and two non-fictional books and saw her becoming an International Best-Selling Author. A woman of resilient courage and high accomplishments, beautifully steered by her soul purpose.

From the Church to Prison

By: Marva Brown-Thomas

"At night when you take off your slippers push them way under the bed so when you have to put them on in the morning you have to get on your knees to reach them. While down there send up a prayer."
Denzel Washington

Born in the small town of Bartlesville to a loving mother and father where we were brought up in the church and was taught about the love of God. My siblings and I were sheltered children and our family dynamics were amazing, a close-knit family. At some point, once I reached an age to sort of make decisions, around 19, I connected with the wrong environment. It was an environment of promiscuity, drinking, a lot of marijuana smoking and a lot of the selling of crack cocaine. This lifestyle had never been set before me, but I felt accepted. I didn't feel totally accepted by church people and a part of me felt that I needed to be accepted. I grew up in silence about a strong lack of self-confidence. In my mind and what I saw, I was a very ugly, black child. To be clear, I wasn't made to feel like that from my family, but kids at school always confirmed what I was seeing; so, I thought! Nonetheless, I gravitated to the streets.

The streets are a mean way of life. It is a life of destruction, jealousy and evil. I was so consumed with being out there. The fast money kept me going with a roof over my head. I truly thought I was living the life. The most embarrassing thing about me selling drugs was that I never built money to have anything to show for it. I found that the old cliché "devil money will not last", to be true. Selling drugs is a way of playing rushing roulette with your life. You are always paranoid about the police finding you out or jealous people setting you up. I can remember at times being the only woman in drug houses with nothing but other men that sold drugs or men and women buying the drugs. My best friend would go from time to time, but not always. My dealer was also a woman, but she had a "stack money" mentality, and she had no need be the actual person on the corners or in the drug house to make money, she was one of the big dealers that small time dealers like myself bought from. I say that to say in my town, you just didn't see very many women selling in the streets during my time out there.

The streets had me consumed. I remember a time I was approached by a guy, who was a dealer, bigger time than myself, asking me to catch a flight from Tulsa, Oklahoma to Los Angeles, California to pick up a kilo of pure powder cocaine and bring it back on the greyhound to Oklahoma. Mind you, I didn't take the time to even think how much danger I was putting myself through. He offered me what he would give me for doing it and I said yes. The things that I did in my past that were not Godly, was before I ever had children so I had the mentality that if anything happened to me, such as getting busted by the police, that I would only be hurting myself. This couldn't have been further from the truth. Whatever in my life hurt me, would hurt my parents for sure, my two baby nephews and my siblings for sure. In the moment, I wasn't thinking like that. With that said, I got on a plane to Los Angeles to pick up a kilo of dope. I had never even laid eyes on that number of drugs. I don't think I was fully aware of the consequences if I were caught. I landed in Los Angeles, the guy that I was picking up the dope for, met us at the airport. I stayed there two days. The next day there we went site seeing, shopping, to the beach and just had a fun time.

The day had come. It was time for me to take a bag of pure powder cocaine, a kilo, which is a lot of dope, and get on a bus all the way across country to deliver for small amount of return. My life, my freedom was on the line until or if, and that's a big if, I made it back to Oklahoma and delivered to the dealer. As we approached the bus depot in Los Angeles, I immediately got paranoid. Where I come from, a small family friendly town, where you catch the bus at a convenient store, one or two people hop on or off and the bus takes off. I was culture shocked at how big this bus depot was. It was almost just as big as LAX (Los Angeles Airport). There were people everywhere. Police and security everywhere. I was trembling from head to toe. The reality at this particular moment was that if there was going to be a drug bust, I was going to be the only one going to prison for a long time. While there was another passenger with me, I had the bag in my possession and was overseeing it the entire time. If you remember, I said earlier that in this game, people will set you up. I had no idea if someone was trying have me set up for the police to bust me or for someone to rob me at gun point. All I knew for certain was, there was no backing out now and if I get busted, there is absolutely no snitching. There is a street code that you live by to be in the dope game and that is you never snitch or there would be life threatening consequences, and mind you, I was one woman dealing with street, gang banging men.

We parked the car, got out, the dealer grabbed the bag of cocaine and immediately handed it to me. At this point, things became silent in my head, though there were hundreds of people all around. It felt like things started moving in slow motion. We walked towards the gate. We got almost right to the gate to enter to find our bus, boom, I dropped the bag on the ground. "I am not doing it," I said. All I remember is hearing the person traveling with me and the dealer saying, "Pick the bag up. Please pick the bag. We are going to get busted, please, please pick the bag up". I stood there for what seemed liked forever, and finally snapped. I knew I had to pick up the bag or I was going to go to jail in Los Angeles, California. Which is a long way from Bartlesville, Oklahoma. I picked up the bag and we proceeded to the bus. She and I got on the bus. I placed the bag on the top compartment in the front of the bus and sat at the very back of the bus. I didn't get any real sleep for watching the bag. We had one bus change and the anxiety kicked back in. I had to touch that bag and transfer it to our next bus which would take us on into Bartlesville. I grabbed the bag and did the same thing. I placed the bag in the front of bus and sat in the back. The next evening, we arrived in Bartlesville at the bus station. One of two things could have happened. When that bus door opened, the police could be waiting or the drug dealer who promised he would be there to get us would be there. Everything in slow motion again, I grabbed the bag, had my co-passenger to go in front of me, I slowly went behind her and here stood, you know who: the drug dealer.

Needless to say, life had changed drastically for me. While he did what he said he was going to do, his life was never on the line. My life was in danger. The only thing that brought me through was the prayers of my mother that carried me the entire time I spent in the streets. I had no regards for my family, who loved me and who I really mattered to. I was searching for the wrong attention. There was no one in the streets telling me to go back home and do what's right. This ultimately led me to prison. While that particular scenario didn't cost me my freedom, I continued to run the streets, sell drugs, do drugs, drink and made life a full party. I was blind to God sending me warning signs and sending my mother to save me. He had to place me in a place where he could get my full attention. I was at my low. I thought I was invincible when I was able to bring drugs across the country safely. No one could have ever told me, growing up, that I would spend time in prison.

While in prison, in the beginning, the devil played with my mind, and all I could think of was getting out to get back to what I was doing. However, God started showing up bigger and broader than the devil. He spoke to me, he said, "I tried to show you things, I sent your mother to save you, but you couldn't hear me, so I had to place you in a position to get your full attention." It was at that point that I grabbed ahold to God's hand and repented for the wrong that I had done. It was at that point that I realized it that I wasn't hurting myself but everyone around me that genuinely cared for me. Most of all it was at that point that I knew life choices had to be different or this wouldn't be the last time I would see jail. I was done hurting my parents, my nephews and myself. I realized that life was more important. My values, my integrity, my freedom meant everything. Most importantly, my relationship with God.

Finally, I have been free from bondage since November 1999. I have never looked back. I value life, family, freedom, and God. Life is what you make it. I hurt people and myself along the way. However, God gave me the opportunity to go back to college to obtain my Bachelor's degree in Business Management and my Master's Degree in Human Resources. He allowed me to create 'Rise Queen' to empower women and their families. There are so many things he has allowed good in my life once I was able to hear him. **Life is a journey of learning and choices. I chose to do the right things even when no one is watching**. The speaking opportunities that I am blessed with is to share my story, my journey. I can't keep it to myself if I want to help others.

BIOGRAPHY: *Marva Brown-Thomas was born and raised in Bartlesville, Oklahoma. Graduated from Bartlesville High School. Attended Oklahoma Wesleyan University where she obtained her Bachelor's in Business Management and her Master's in Human Resources. Employed with Phillips 66 Company for 16 years. She is a wife to her living husband Frank Thomas* and a mother to her amazing children Martae' Brown-Hill and A'nia Brown-Hill. Marva is the creator of Rise Queen a Women's Empowerment Conference where her loving mother, Linda Brown, is the President of Operations. She is also CEO/Founder, Chief Editor of Black Link Magazine as well as a published Author. Her main asset is that she is a child of God and a lover of her family. She adores her home church Greater First Baptist where she sings in the choir. She dedicates all her achievements to her late father Roy F. Brown, Sr. RIP Daddy! "God first in all that I do," Marva Brown-Thomas.

19

Made It Through

Myechia Barnett

"For I know the plans I have for you,' declares the Lord, 'plans to prosper you and not to harm you, plans to give you a hope and a future." Jeremiah 29:11

Have you ever been so afraid of something that you feel like you should run from it? Rather than face it you get out of dodge. We think sometimes moving to a new state or city, even across the country, that our problems will go away but they do not.

At the age of 17-18 years old, I was in an abusive relationship with someone a little younger than me. Imagine being in a room isolated with him right next to you. You cannot leave the room unless he goes with you. You cannot go to the bathroom without him being there with you or even bathe. A conversation leads to you being punched in the face because this is the only person, you are sexual with but in his mind, he checks your v*****a as if he is not. He honestly believes that.

Your anxiety is so high so you spend most of your time at the hospital for them to tell you that they cannot find anything. Is this your escape route?

See I did not truly understand what was happening to me, because of the lies of those around me that accepted it, seemed normal. He loves me, he does not understand what he is doing. Maybe, he did not. It was normal for him because that is all he knew from those around him.

Here it goes again but this time, the fight led to outside. He is constantly accusing you anyway, so you feed into it.... "Yes! I'm having sex with someone else, is that what you want to hear!?" (WAP) He struck me in the face with a 2-piece and we started fighting. Blood dripping from my lip, it is dark outside, I can see the other houses and no one else to come rescue me. The people who were living in the same home with us was outside but what did they do? Nothing. (Sirens) The police show up and even though I wanted to protect him, I could not. My face told the story they needed to arrest him. They take me to the station and ask me questions. What do we do as women experiencing this...? Deny it? Right? But why? They gave me a mirror and tears could not stop falling. Who is this girl? She is no longer pretty. Her beautiful face is not as it was. Her eye is black and swollen. Her lips are bleeding and swollen as well.

I paint this picture to tell you I know. To be completely honest, this is The Lord because I was not going to share this story because I'm writing it in my book. What I will tell you is... eventually I did run away.

I did move in with my grandmother. I tried to stop talking to him but ended right back for a split moment because now my mind is on getting out of the state or far away to keep me from being able to easily access him or for him to access me. Long story short, I experienced suicidal thoughts and proceeded to act upon them, and one day a light bulb blew up in me and I said, "Enough is enough."

I ended up leaving him because I had no choice, I had to. Me nor my son deserved that. My son did not deserve to experience or witness this turmoil, regardless of young he was. I tried to get myself together and ended up with another man to get away from the one I was running from. I ended up pregnant for him, and then I went back grandma house I go.

One day, at a family house, we talked about things and how my mom and aunt moved to Georgia. Internally, I think, "I am going because I don't have anything here anyway. Why not start over somewhere where no one knows you?" Externally, I did not want my sons growing up in the streets. I really did not want that, but truth be told, I was running from that boy. Mentally, there was a battle because some women still love men, regardless of what men do to us.

Aren't you a queen?

Don't you deserve better?

There is always a way out, we must decide to take the road out.

Unfortunately, some victims of domestic violence choose to stay. My sister if you are reading this.... *Only you can decide what is for best for you.*

I am here to tell you it is not easy. Life is challenging. Circumstances make us hurt. Let us decide to take care bad situations, because not doing so will cause future things to happen if they are not dealt with sooner, I pray that you get counseling or therapy. I was saved in April 2009 and moved to Georgia in September 2009 with nothing but my clothes and my son, while pregnant with another. All I could think was "Thank You Father for making a way out for me and children, externally. During those times, I cried out many times to God, still do. I remember praying and did not understand why He did not help me. I went through all of that and more. But God was always there for me. God is right there with you now. No matter the circumstances.

I hear God saying, "They did it to me too." The difference is we are not Him; we strive to be like Him. Your best days are ahead of you queen. Decide for you and your children if you have any. Our past does not control us unless we allow it to.

My story did stop in Georgia .... I made it through.

BIOGRAPHY: I am a serial-preneur with the intention to help others. I am a coach, publisher, best-selling international author, web designer and more. While I wear many hats, my intentions are legacy and to help others obtain theirs.

National Suicide Prevention Lifeline 800-273-8255 Hours: Available 24 hours. Languages: English, Spanish. **National Domestic Violence Hotline** The Hotline can be accessed via the nationwide number **1-800-799-SAFE (7233)**

20

The Balancing Act: How I Overcame and Found Peace

By: Nova Speaks

My journey of motherhood started unexpectedly and without warning, I woke one day, six months into my pregnancy, to find that I was going into spontaneous labor. The shock of the discovery was overridden by the concern for my child's wellbeing. My son was born three months premature, weighing two pounds and eight ounces. I lovingly called him "the little boy", with his legal name carrying the meaning

"The Strong One". His name fit him exactly right in the sense that he overcame the odds placed against him with a mysterious internal strength.

At two months and a half, he suffered a brain hemorrhage. The doctors gave it time to see if his brain would heal on its own, but it resulted with him being diagnosed with a condition, hydrocephalus, otherwise known as "water on the brain". Meaning the natural fluids produced to safeguard his brain could no longer be processed by his body alone. He had to have a shunt implanted, a medical device needed for his survival, to drain this fluid to prevent build up and pressure that would cause him to go into a life-threatening state. I still recall the look in the surgeon's eyes as I asked when it could be removed, and she informed me it would be a part of him for life. I know now that this is a fairly common condition, but at the time, it felt like another obstacle that would keep my son from having options in life. The surgeon showed great kindness to me, and he was sent to me from above, taking the time to comfort me as I processed the news.

The months spent in the NICU were slow paced, each day an opportunity for something new to go wrong, but mostly, things went right enough. My son grew and flourished while under care, and soon enough he was able to go home when he met the necessary requirements.

The hospital released him the day before my twenty-first birthday, the best birthday gift I will have ever received in my life. I was raised under the religion of Jehovah's Witnesses, which gave me a childhood without traditional celebrations. And so, on a birthday that is usually celebrated by many as the right to legally drink alcohol, I stepped happily into the full-time role of motherhood without regret.

In a way, he was a typical child. He liked to be held. In fact, once we were reunited, he would not sleep unless he was firmly placed on top of my heart. (I like to think he missed the sound of it during our four-month separation and was happy to be home.) He liked most toys and would spend his time trying to learn to clutch his hands around their curves and edges. It took a few months for me to accept that he was in fact any different than any other child, the hope in my heart intertwining with my denial. At first, he seemed like a normal baby from what I read in baby books. Between six to eight months is when I noticed the main differences and consulted with his pediatrician on what could be done to support his development.

Again, I was met with a list of milestones he should be meeting. I was directed towards Early Childhood Intervention programs, and the advice given was to "wait, practice and see."

By the age of one he was diagnosed with a non-verbal speech delay, physical and mental delays. Alongside his premature status, autism and cerebral palsy would join the list in the years to come. His future was filled with unknown possibilities, it seemed the medical professionals were attempting to prepare me for a life of hardships and then placed him solely in my care and on my way.

With an extensive list of resources and doctor appointments, I tried to make sense of a world I had never thought I would enter. I know the doctors may have seen countless cases before ours and felt it best to err on the side of caution, rather than give false hope of things to come. Perhaps in my own grief, I could only hear the negatives, as fear was becoming a close friend since finding out my happy-ever-after was not going to be what I had once hoped. So, as time went by, I thought to myself.

"Ok then. If we cannot talk to each other, let us sing."

While the doctors and therapist knew him by his medical history in comparison to the growth of others with his conditions, I knew him best by his bond with me. My little one had no patience for lullabies and would cry if I tried to sing "Mary had a little lamb" to him, he preferred songs sung in my natural voice. "I Never," by Rilo Kiley, became our song as I would dance with him around the room. Daily tasks had songs assigned with lyrics matching what needed to be done. Some songs my own, some given to me by the therapists that worked with him as he grew.

Over time, he sang back to me, matching tune, and pitch. Over time I slowed the pace and matched it closer to speech patterns, and so he did the same, and so his "nonverbal" status developed into more of a mimic style of speech. His teachers and therapist enjoyed the challenge as well, being more used to adapting to the needs of an individual child than I. This trait became part of his nature, to sing when communicating. It became part of the joy of having him as a part of life.

And so, I chose to adapt to each part of him just the same.

At an age where most parents were encouraging their child to crawl towards them, I was placing my son on his side and speaking to him behind his ear so he would be tempted to look over his shoulder at me. He would roll over without meaning to, and I would just laugh and encourage him that he was safe. The look of worry left his eyes and he quickly adapted to finding this mode of transportation fun. He never really did learn how to crawl, but he would roll down the hall and around his room and eventually started reaching for things. Those around him would try to grab his hand and help him stand but he would pull away, upset by the attempt to assist him. Independence seemed to be a common theme as he developed. Years passed by working on small steps. Every achievement was proof of growth. Slowly he even started feeding himself by hand, still struggling with using a fork and knife.

With consideration of his implanted life support in response to his hydrocephalus, there was not much to adapt to, but much to accept. I remember a night he rolled off the couch, which would seem innocent enough of a mistake of a new parent, felt to me like a travesty. I called the nurses hotline provided by his doctors. Cradling him in my arms, afraid he was dying while I watched on. The nurse asked me what he was doing, and I answered that he had cried for a moment but was back to sleep now. I could hear her smile as she said that she thought he was ok; the fall would not do enough damage to the machinery to cause any harm. She asked me if I knew the symptoms of a shunt failure and I recited to her by memory the signs I look for every day. She said if he started having symptoms to bring him in. I hung up the phone and held him all night until morning. He was fine. I relayed the details to his specialist and pediatrician at his next visit who assured me just the same, with a smile. With this, I had to learn to accept that this condition did not make him as fragile as an egg. My son was not humpty dumpty, there would not be any "couldn't put him back together again" moment for me. I relaxed as a mother a little bit after that.

As the years passed and most of my fears of my son's conditions and quality of life abated, I decided to pursue my journey of motherhood further. I myself grew up with siblings and did not want to keep him from having the joy I had experienced firsthand.

And at age 3, the little boy was standing suddenly in the grass of the back yard, he paused and looked at a world he had not seen without the aid of others. He stood without anyone asking him to, without hands stretched out to him. My son took his first steps purely on his own. His determination was a beautiful aspect of his spirit. As I watched him stand on his own two feet for the first time solo, my faith grew that he would one day be strong enough to walk his path through life alone too.

When the little boy stood tall in the grass and took his first steps, my new man was sitting next to me, holding my hand, keeping me from making a sound and distracting the little boy from his mission, whispering to me "See, he did it." He kissed the back of my hand as we looked on. His other hand was on my stomach, which held our first daughter as she grew. We were now renting our first house together; a positive pregnancy test confirmed our growing family three weeks after we moved in.

After I had our first daughter, at two months old, I looked into her little grumpy face, and I knew she needed a sister of her own. Their dad asked me if I was sure and then excitedly agreed. I trusted my inner knowing and sure enough, my second daughter was born a year and two months after the first. Having three children under the age of five, that part of life has multiple stories of its own, filled with sleepless nights and sweet moments of watching them grow into their sibling bond.

At first the little boy was so confused, he did not know what a baby was, even after seeing strangers with them, this was the first one of his own. Watching his sister take her first step, he just stared as she crawled and then climbed and then walked. When she spoke for the first time, he did a double take, astonished that she was capable of speech. He smiled and clapped along with us for her, cheering her on, as he watched us do. She would lay down next to him for a nap and take his little hand in hers. He had to learn to look out for her, already used to being the only one in our care, we often had to move her out of his path as he walked around her. Over time the little boy learned and reminded himself, saying "be careful of the baby" each time he saw her, mimicking our words of caution.

I never know if he remembers his own time doing just the same but watching him see her become a little human was a highlight of that time. Watching her go to her brother and hug him without restraint, without judgement, was a healing moment to all involved.

I worried less that he would have a life without love, for his sisters loved him without a concern that he was different. He seemed happier than before, having little ones to watch as he grew. Their presence showed him the way.

By the time his second sister was born, he knew what to expect. He whispered "sister" the day he met her and leaned in to kiss her on her forehead, happy to have another partner in crime. His smile added to the joy in the room. Acceptance was in his nature, and it seemed to me he was built to love.

And those girls, they were built to show him how to be a child and a big brother. We baby proofed the house in ways we never had to before, the little boy never much bothered to get into things an A-typical child would. But the girls, they were another matter and he loved to help them. So, when they couldn't open the door due to the baby proof tools designed to keep them safe, he learned by watching us open the doors with this contraption on it and would open the door for them. He laughed as we chased after them, watching them run free. And they loved to return the favor, if he would open the fridge, they would pick out the best foods. If he would only turn on the water hose for them, they would show him how to play in the sprinkler. They became a tightly knitted crew, finding their own adventures to get into together.

As time went by, they grew stronger into their own personalities. Now we are at a point where the struggles of the beginning were well worth it. He is 11 years old now and still fighting to reach milestones that may possibly be out of reach for him. Only time will tell.

Now I look at my three children, we have gone through numerous struggles. So many great memories between the beginning and where we are now. Each day presents its own challenges to face and new opportunities for us to grow as individuals and as a family.

My daughters are bright eyed and spontaneous, they look after their brother in a two-pronged attack style. The older is the protector who keeps him from harm's way with a roar, challenging anything that would threaten him. The younger is the loving nurse, calming his episodes with a smile and a hand to hold. How he loves his sisters, and they love him, it is perfection at its finest.

My daughters and I have deep talks about life in general, their future, their fears and hopes, and mine as well. Conversations that remind me of the time I spent with my own mother before her passing. Often, I will repeat her words of wisdom, and add in ones of my own. More often my children surprise me with their thoughts and outlooks on life. We talk about what we think their brother is thinking at any moment, giving him a voice to match his moods while he still learns to communicate more effectively with those around him.

My son is strong and funny and the sweetest boy one could ever hope to meet. We continue to adapt to his needs together. Our bond keeps us sane as we soldier on. Our memories remind us how far we have come. Each of us helps the other through rough days bit by bit. We fight and argue. We love one another. As I realize we are really only one third of the way through this journey, of raising kids to become adults, my only hope is that I help them find their way to become who they are truly meant to be. What I have already learned so far is how little they need me, how they will be just fine. I see in the distance a brighter future than the one I once feared to be possible.

I still sing Rilo Kiley, "I Never", as I hold my tall eleven-year-old boy, but now, we sing it together. He runs when once we were told he would not walk. He still speaks in a mimic fashion, repeating phrases that others have said to him, or he has learned in passing. I still worry for the future, but no longer for him. He is brave in ways that no doctor could have ever foretold. He learns step by step and with repetition and is trying to be as independent as he can. He has learned to ask for help when he needs to.

My oldest daughter is a firecracker, speeding through life without care for consequences. Her smile is mischievous and filled with secrets. Her soul is that of a warrior, ready for action and daring the world to try her. She was built to be a protector and, as far as I know, would never let harm come to any of her siblings, not if she is around to stop it.

My youngest, beautifully kind and softer than a newborn kitten. She thinks of others before herself, a natural caregiver. Her smile will brighten anyone's day, I dare you to try to stay sad in her presence, she will quickly find a way to turn your day around.

As my mother would say about the children she raised. What shocked her most is how different we all were from each other. So, I embrace that about my own little family. Each piece of us is different, but like puzzle pieces, we fit together. Oddly enough, in this day and age, the puzzle piece is a symbol of an autistic child. They fit in exactly where they are meant to if you give them half a chance.

And this is the story of how I overcame the balancing of my fears and hopes. I found my way to what matters, loving those who love you. Life always has a way of balancing out.

With love, always ~Nova Speak

BIOGRAPHY: *Nova spent her childhood as an Army Brat and in services of her mother's ministry, leading to a walk of life where she encountered people of different faiths and upbringings, with a joy installed in her of connecting with others. Nova has since grown into the full-time role of motherhood, as well as caregiver to her eldest, a child who lives a life under special considerations. Specializing in rising up when life knocks one down to become the true version of herself, accepting and embracing the challenges of life as an opportunity to* grow. Nova has lived a life with enough reasons to feel defeated and has found a way to see the silver lining in all things. Writing under the pen name of "Nova Speaks" in place of her legal name, serves as symbolism of her journey, and reminder to speak up for oneself in order to fully embrace their place in this world. Nova is here in the hopes that she can help others find their way.

21

What He Left Behind

By: Dr. Pamela J. Edwards

"If you can imagine it, you can achieve it. If you can dream it, you can become it." --William Arthur Ward

He was the love of my life. And, honestly, he still is.

Andre and I were married for 30 wonderful, amazing years. Our journey began in 1991 when we met at a club in the Acres Homes area of Houston called Sid's Ranch. I was in a toxic relationship with a boyfriend who had broken up with me, yet again, until he decided he wanted to come back. I was tired of the games and ready to move on. My friends convinced me to go to the club with them and have a good time. I totally was not the clubbing type, but that night, I figured I might as well. Didn't have anything else better to do anyway.

We piled into the car and went to Sid's Ranch. I was just a few days from my 21st birthday, so the guy who was checking I.D. at the door of the club allowed me to go in. Well, since I wasn't the clubbing type, I was the one who was at the table watching everybody's drinks while they went to dance. I'm sitting there, happened to turn around, and a guy was sitting directly at the next table, looking at me and smiling. I gave a little smile, then turned back around. I was shy and didn't know if this guy was a perve or not.

He tried to strike up a conversation with me, but it was so loud in the club that I couldn't hear him, so we went outside and stood by his car and talked. As I got to know him, I liked the fact that he was a hard worker (he was a restaurant manager) and definitely had goals in his life. He also had a healthy respect for God, unlike many of the guys I ran into who would often curse His name, which is an immediate turn-off for me.

He gave me his number, and we talked a few times. However, I ended up losing contact with him for several months. I remember looking in the Yellow Pages for the restaurant he worked. There were approximately twenty locations listed, so I called each one of them until I located him. Once I found him, he said he was so happy to hear from me, and he was bragging about me to his family. He called me "The Good Girl," because I wouldn't sit in his car with him nor hold his hand that night, he met me at the club. From that point, we started dating.

The thing that really let me know that Andre was the one was when I got extremely sick with pericarditis, which is inflammation of the lining of the heart (yes, it is as painful as it sounds, and very debilitating). It is a condition that I was afflicted with several times a year. Where other guys walked away when I got sick, he took me into his home, took care of me, took me to hospitals to seek out treatment, cooked for me, read the Bible with me, and prayed for me. He did this for me every day for the 4-6 weeks the attacks would last, each and every time they occurred.

We got married in 1994 and had a son. We had such wonderful, memorable moments as a family, as well as challenges that we overcame. We lived in our old community for well over a decade, then moved to a new community in 2005. We continued to love, enjoy our lives, and reach great heights of success in so many areas.

Then, in June 2021, the Lord called my sweetheart home to be with Him. I know that life is not forever, but this is the hardest, most agonizing experience I have ever had to go through. Though I am healing slowly, I still have pain deep in my soul every day. The reality of his ultimate absence is unimaginable.

I am finding comfort and healing in a number of ways that I hope will be helpful to those reading.

For starters, though his body is in the grave and his soul is in Heaven, his essence is everywhere in the house. I still smell his scent in our home because most of his clothes and shoes are in the areas where he left him until when, and if, I decide to donate them.

I look at the pictures of our life together. He had the most beautiful hazel eyes I have ever seen.

I took two of his rings and I wear one on a chain as a necklace inside of my shirt, the other I put on my key ring. I still wear my wedding ring, too. I'm not ready to take that off yet.

I listen to compilations that he created of his favorite songs.

I still have the text messages he sent to me over the years. Every morning, he would text a message to me, saying, "Good Morning, Princess," or, "Good Morning, my precious wife." These, and others, I have printed and hung in special places in my home as a reminder of the love that he left behind.

I treasure the gifts he bought me over the years, especially his last gifts. For our anniversary (Valentine's Day), he bought me a crown and a golden heart necklace with our names engraved upon it. For my birthday, he bought items with paintings created by my favorite artist, Thomas Kincade.

Sometimes, when I really, really miss him, I listen to the recordings I made on my phone of some of the conversations we would have. I have also transferred copies of these recordings to my email accounts, Google Drive, my YouTube page, and other applications, to have extra copies to access just in case some get lost for whatever reason. Being able to hear his voice in this way, as well as watching a few videos I was able to get (he didn't like being recorded, so I had to sneak and do these) help me to get through another day. As time goes by, I find that I have the need to listen a little bit less, just every once in a while. I take that as a sign that I am healing and learning to remember him without pain.

I remember the very wise advice that he gave me in life. He was not only a good family leader, but also a good reader of people and securer of resources. His advice and referrals are helping me to run our house and business to this day.

As I move forward in my life post-marriage, I am so excited about what is to come. I continue to rediscover myself, expand Edwards Consulting, the business we both started, and seek out new, exciting opportunities. No matter what, I know that because #LoveNeverDies, Andre will always be a special part of my life. I will hold him in my heart until God allows us to be together again for all time. Until then, I embrace and treasure the everlasting love he left behind.

I love you, Andre. You will always be the love of my life.

Until we unite again...

BIOGRAPHY: *Dr. Pamela J. Edwards is a professor, patient accounts specialist, freelance writer, and ordained in ministry. She lives in Houston, Texas.*

22

When I Learned to Love

By: Precious Swain-Peaks

Bright lights, machines wailing, and nurses moving quickly while the doctor shouts orders.

"We cannot wait any longer, we have to do a cesarean before you have a stroke" was the last thing I heard.

I wake up alone, I touch my stomach. Before I could scream, as if she heard my thoughts, the nurse came in. In an instance my life had changed.

Nineteen years before, a baby girl was born. Not really sure if she would live, babies born early didn't make it through during that time. They put her in the incubator under the lights and hoped for the best. Born to a heroin addicted mother, the pains of withdrawal had to have been horrible, but she made it.

The apple of her grandparent's eye, she was their princess. Her extreme intelligence covered her personality disorder well. Even when it was time for school the lack of social skills was attributed to only child syndrome.

Time would reveal there was a much darker source.

The mother she had never seen makes an awarding winning appearance when she turns six. Any hopes of normalcy were postponed. The pain inflicted by her mother destroyed any ability to bond with people that may have been left.

Children of addicted parents are considered easy targets. Get the parent high and the child is open game. Album covers, lines of powder, needles, and small tied unblown up balloons were the warning signs to hide. The closet, the cabinet, the car, even the dark scary garage were places to hide from the painful touches of random hands.

Like a rerun of an episode from an ABC After School Special every Friday the show would play over. Everyone would meet up, they would all get high, the heroin addicts would lean, and the cocaine addicts would do insane things. I believe the music dictated the mood. Some days they would fight, other times their nasty fantasies came to life wherever they were. No matter how beautiful the women were, how open to the interaction, or how flirtatious they appeared there was one person that waited for things to get started and when everyone was in their zone he would come where the kids were.

If everyone was at her mother's house, she would be the sole target. He would spit in his hand and manipulate himself while licking her private parts until his fluid came forth. If everyone had met at her mother's friend's house around the corner, he would make her friend lick her private parts while he entered her crying friend. Afterwards these two traumatized little girls would cry together, and the older girl would always apologize for hurting her; telling her when she got big to run away.

The body is a very confusing entity. Something can hurt really bad but feel so good all at the same time. Imagine the confusion felt by a child; scared, angry, confused, while not understanding why this thing that she hated gave a strange sense of pleasure.

The only people she ever felt a connection to were no longer able to protect her, she had no connection with the woman that was naturally her mother. Between her mother's physical/verbal abuse, and the sexual abuse she encountered at the hands of those who called her their niece the ability to smile was gone.

At twelve she was caught selling marijuana at school, to avoid child neglect charges her mother declared her incorrigible. For six long months she was bounced between the juvenile facility and the group homes. No one could really understand how a child so gifted had found themselves in such a situation. She never told anyone the things that she experienced or even that the marijuana she was caught with was her mothers.

Upon release she went to live with her other set of grandparents. Her nightmares of killing her mother caused them to take her for counseling. Diagnosed with Nymphomania and Reactive Attachment Disorder, both of which they said could be treated but not cured.

It all began to make sense to the people around her why though she seemed genuinely appreciative for anything that was done for her in a cold scary way she seemed to not care.

If she saw you, she saw you, if she didn't it didn't matter.

No long after going back to live with her mother, and the death of her father, she walked away and never looked back. It wasn't easy but the things she had been through taught her to survive and from fifteen to seventeen she lived on her own. She never quit school, she never sold her body, and she survived.

During her senior year of high school, she met a young man a year older than her. His mother had no daughters and instantly took to her. She and the young man got married.

Sadly, not for love. Not even for like, none of that mattered to her at all. They got married out of convenience. She was able to take a break, focus on school, and not have to concern herself with how bills would be paid. To him it seemed normal, she cooked, cleaned, and had lots of sex. He didn't realize that sex for her had nothing to do with love it was simply to quench the desire for the feeling. She cleaned because she hated a dirty environment and she cooked because she was hungry.

He never understood that when she attempted suicide it was because she was tired. She wasn't angry, she wasn't depressed, she was simply tired. Tired of being different. Tired of living the way she was living. Tired of watching people who seemed so happy and said it was because they were in love but not being able to feel that way too.

When she found out she was pregnant it was a surprise. She had been told she would never be able to have children. She wasn't sure if she was happy or not. The first time the baby kicked there was a feeling that came over her. The more the baby grew, the more he moved the more she felt an emotion that was new to her. This was part of her. This was something that was her responsibility.

During the labor process she told the doctor if a choice had to be made let her die so her baby could live. Immediately panic set in when she awoke with no child.

When the nurse brought him in, and she saw him for the first time she knew she was in love. He looked just like her. He needed her. He was the greatest gift.

That she is me. My first son changed my life. He was the first person I ever truly loved. He taught me how to care about how someone else felt. He was the best thing that I never knew I needed.

I have seven natural children, each that I love unconditionally. They brought more children that strangely I loved like my own. My ability to attach to other adults was a struggle that I really never truly mastered, until the Most High set me apart by myself to see the ugly, broken, little girl that I was in a grown woman's body. He allowed me to see that my marriages failed because they weren't based on love but instead based on other selfish things. None were to men sent by him, instead they were to men I thought were the one because of something they had going on. He showed me that my hatred for women came directly from my situation with my mother but that it was unfair to judge others based on her.

He showed me that I treated men as sex objects but that was wrong.

He showed me how my inability to trust people had a negative effect on my business.

He showed me that I could forgive myself, there was nothing I could have done to stop the things that were happening, and that my mother's addiction was not my fault.

In that I found the real me, the minister, the mother, the wife, the sister, the friend, the businesswoman. Not just a survivor but an OVERCOMER.

No matter where you come from and what you have been through remember these words: *"For I know the thoughts that I think toward you, saith YAHUAH, thoughts of peace, and not of evil, to give you an expected end."*

BIOGRAPHY: *Precious Swain-Peaks is an Accountant /Business Consultant;1X International Best Seller; 2X Best-selling Author; Global Speaker/ Educator; Owner of Swain Girl Media a multimedia publishing company and home iMakeStarz Digital Broadcasting Network; Owner of Anointed For Prosperity Bookkeeping and More; Founder of New Visions Ministries of Florida, Inc.; With over 30yrs experience helping business owners build a strong foundation and gain financial growth. Anointedforprosperity.com IG: @anointedforprosperity*

23

Sis, Just Leap!

By: Raven J. Williams

As I stood on the ledge looking down at the valley below, all I could do was wonder, "What led me to this point?". My heart is racing at full speed, my anxiety is on high, and the anticipation of the unknown now sits at the forefront of every thought and emotion within me. How in the world did I get into this overwhelming situation?

I then turned my head slightly over my left shoulder and began to think back to all the obstacles, setbacks, and people who pushed and shoved and chased me to point of standing on the edge. Now that I'm here, I ask myself, what do I do?

If I take another step forward, will I fall in the deep valley or will that step be large enough to get me to the other side. A side that I've never seen, a side unknown, yet a side that could be filled with possibilities, opportunities, and countless life changing wins.

At this point, I knew that before I could think about what was ahead of me, I had to make the hard decision to do something about the things that led me to this point.

I was so nervous about moving forward because of what lied in the valley below. All I could feel was the pain, the rejection, and the unhelpful influences of those who were supposed to help me yet turned out to only want to call out my name to seek personal gain. What if I took another step forward and fell back down in the low valley and ended up right back where I started, then ultimately thinking of this same decision... on the ledge again?

Let me start at the beginning, and take you back about twenty years, as I introduce myself. My name is Raven Williams and I'd like to share my journey of Purpose, the Process, and the Promise, which ultimately helped me to decide on what to do.

The Purpose

This entire life that I have lived has been led, lived, and breathed through purpose. Once I understood what my gift was and the unique passion that I had to inspire others, I knew that I was walking in my purpose. You see part of my personal mission is to push and inspire others believe when they do not have the strength to believe in themselves. I could only do that from experience, hard lessons, and a willing spirit to seek, learn, and position myself to reach the masses. Everything that I have gone through in life, prepared me for each moment ahead. I had no idea that my journey could or would be as like others journey until I was purposely positioned in places to meet and mentor others. From strategy to implementation, I have been on a mission to fulfill my purpose of *"Transforming lives, one conversation at a time"*. This is simply what I do, and what I've been shown as my purpose.

The Process

Understanding my purpose was rather easy for me but going through the process was the total opposite. Until I was reminded of what processing meant.

Have you ever been introduced to an idea that was so amazing that you could not wait to jump on board? For me it was not just one idea, but it was several ideas that I jumped on board with, prematurely, because I just wasn't ready. I had to learn the hard way to make sure that I was personally prepared mentally and physically for the journey ahead. In other words, I was trying to process my journey before it was time and that is never a good thing. So, I often reminded myself that I had to wait and let things bake. Oh yes, did I mention that I love to move around the kitchen? So, I often connect my journey with the process of waiting when cooking. If you take something out of the oven while it's still in its baking (processing) phase, then it's not going to be ready to eat. Such is the same with life. And sis, I'll share with you what I've learned, which is that *everything that we have cooking in life is going to be amazing, but only after it's been processed and ready for consumption by the world.*

The processing phase will take you out of that normality phase. The processing phase will allow you time to marinate, meditate and immerse yourself deeper into a deeper level that only you and God could understand. Going into that deeper level will allow you to connect to a power source that is so strong that all those around you will feel the radiance from around you. You see, when you are connected, then everything that you touch, every path that you cross, every life that you sow into, and every person whom you mentor will be connected to that source and win, but only after you have gone deeper in your processing phase.

The other thing that I have learned in this processing phase is that everything has a season. Things may not happen when you would like for it to happen, and if that is you, then understand that it's still processing.

You may pray for something in the spring season, and wonder why in the wintertime, you still have not received exactly what you've prayed for but understand that it's still processing. One thing I have learned is that what you pray for may not happen in your scheduled season, but it will happen in due season. And if God assured you that it will happen, it doesn't matter what is happening during your processing season, He always makes it happen in His timing, which is your due season, which you will know exactly when it is. Which leads me to the Promise.

The Promise

You see, as I stood on that ledge that I told you about, waiting, watching, and wondering, I remembered his promise to me. I share this story everywhere I go, which is God personally whispered the following to me. He said:

No matter where you go, or what you do, remember that I am always with you, therefore you will never be alone. Any time you get afraid, anxious, or feel lost, look to the left, then look to the right. There you will find two friends, affectionately called "Grace" and "Mercy"; and as long as you let me guide you, you will never be alone. You will always make it to the other side. You will always win.

So as I stood on that ledge, after looking over my left shoulder at what was ahead, I turned my head slightly back to my direct side and was reminded of Grace, then I looked to the right, and was reminded of Mercy, then I no longer wanted to look down in the valley, yet I looked ahead and knew that all I had to do was take a step forward to be guided in the right direction. At that moment, with my head held high... I LEAPED ... and made it to the other side. Yes, I made it over and I can now confidently reintroduce myself to the world and say that I am an accomplished, award-winning author, speaker, publisher, magazine owner, internationally recognized businesswoman, master leadership trainer for corporate and non-profit organizations, mentor, and purpose-pusher.

I am also here to encourage you to take the leap, remember the words that were spoken to me as if they were shared with you also. Don't let anyone or anything that's not connected to the source enter your atmosphere or cause you to look back or down with anxiety. Connect yourself with winning people who are ready to help you move forward. There's nothing that you can't do. I made it over, and so can you.

24

Overcoming Someone Else's Addiction -When Crack Cocaine is the Mistress

"To Thine Own Self Be True"

By: Sheree Alison Casey

My story is about how I survived being married to a man with a very serious addiction to crack cocaine. But, unfortunately, the relationship to crack cocaine consumed his life and became his permanent lover.

After the failure of my first marriage, I became a single parent of four children. Once they became teenagers, I did not feel the need to jump into a serious relationship, so I made a sacrifice and chose to throw myself in my work. So, I only dated casually.

As the years went by, tragedy struck, and my only daughter had succumbed to cancer at the age of eighteen, leaving behind her infant son of whom I became guardian. At the time, my youngest was about to start college, and this was around the time that I connected with the man that would soon become my second husband. As a born-again believer with a strong Christian faith, I had just received my license in ministry and desired to do everything right according to the word of God. I prayed, laid before God while shut in at the church. I also sought Godly council from my Pastor.

I did everything that I knew how to do. I wanted to be sure that this time things would work out, because another failed marriage was not an option. Statistics show that in the United States, 50% percent of first-time marriages, 67% of second marriages, and 74% of third marriages end in divorce. (Smith, Sept.2021) I waited a long time to consider remarry so I needed to do things correctly. Somehow, I believed that it would be better than the first failed marriage. Little did I know that this one would be my most memorable ride.

Our relationship began slowly; he saw me with my friends one night at a party where his band was playing and had remembered me from high school over 40 years ago. I had not seen nor heard anything about him nor his life after high school. A close friend told me that he was asking about me. At first, I was hesitant, and thought, "I don't really know him." I was in my hometown visiting with my mom in New Jersey, as I resided in Arizona. My friend gave him my phone number, and he started calling me on Sunday afternoons. He was always polite and respectful, and talked about God, the church, and his aspirations for ministry. He was also a musician, and the love of music was something we had in common. As we shared each other's dreams, we became close, we talked almost every day. I thought that he was an answer to my prayer because he had no children and could help me raise my grandson. He stated that it would be an honor for him because he was not blessed with the opportunity to have a child naturally.

We continued to build a long-distance relationship that lasted over a year. We soon began to discuss me returning to New Jersey so that we could get married and build a life together. Then one day, he said that he would be willing to move to Arizona to start a life with me. He told me that he had discussed his plans with his Pastor and that he was given the blessing to move forward.

When entering into a second marriage or a relationship these days, you have to ask questions. I admit that I was so smitten that someone (a man) would move across the country for me that I was so blindsided that I ignored the red flags right in front of me. I made assumptions based on my lifestyle. He had told me that he had been struggling with addiction for many years and that he had been clean and sober for the last two. Soon after, I found out that this was not true. The other part of that was he had no solid work history. I could never imagine anyone not working or having responsibilities being past the age of 50.

When he arrived in Arizona, we sat down with my Pastor, and he was asked several questions that pertained to him providing and caring for my grandson and me, in the interest of protecting me. After we completed our sessions, we planned our wedding. The idea of being married again was euphoric for me.

Two months later, things began to change when I noticed that money and other things started missing out the house. He sold my camera that had the last pictures of my daughter on the memory card. That became my reality check that I had married a crack addict. With his addiction, he could not keep a steady job. I had to hide my purse, jewelry, and bankcard. Every time we left on Sunday morning for church, I would notice the neighbors staring at me. I soon realized they were the drug dealers that he bought his crack from.

Friends told me that I should have walked away, but I could not because, we all come to the table with baggage, if I can be honest. My baggage was – I could not take the humiliation, guilt, and shame or the thought of failure associated with this situation. It was a gut-wrenching and embarrassing time for me. I felt that for me to be in this situation as a minister in the church and an educated woman with a master's degree who works with addicts was the ultimate catastrophe.

For an African American man to come all the way from the east coast to marry me was quite a big deal, and my husband wasn't bad looking and was very well dressed. I soon found out later that it was worse than I thought. He had been borrowing money from my close friends behind my back to get high. It was also discovered he had never had his own place and had been living from rehab to rehab. In reflection, I take responsibility because I should have been asking these important questions. I made assumptions that he had been honest with me. Sadly, that was not the case. Every few months, when he was sober, he would get a job. I would breathe and get comfortable because there were two incomes, but then he would disappear with the money from his paycheck. This behavior happened consistently for about four or five years, and I ended up taking the fall for it. During this time, he went to several rehabs, which was the only time I felt relieved. The longest time he stayed away was for a year, but afterwards things would go right back where they were within a few weeks. It was during this time I began to get tired and weary. Every time I addressed something suspicious, he would gaslight me and tell me that I was imaging things, and that I did not trust him. He was right about me not trusting him. Our church was trying to be supportive and was in constant prayer for us.

By the time the sixth year came, I had had enough. I knew that I had to provide for my grandson, so I went back to school to obtain my Masters. Under all of that stress I made it. I had begun to check out emotionally because the uncertainty had drained me. I was diagnosed with high blood pressure and became depressed. At times I felt over-whelmed. But overall, I was always embarrassed and ashamed. I could not share this situation with my friends or family. I suddenly realized that I was not happy and found myself praying for a way out.

I started working multiple jobs all the time, so I would not have to be at home. I planned vacations and went with friends. I would not leave my grandchild with him because at this point, I no longer trusted his judgment. The finale came when he begged me to get him a job at the agency where I worked. This job paid really well, but he messed that up after a month. It became the beginning of the end for me. He had blown the entire month's rent in one night. It was at that moment I asked him to leave; he was all set to go and suddenly became ill and had to be taken to the hospital. He was diagnosed with something called White lung pneumonia. It was kind of like COVID. And he had to be placed on a ventilator. I had to deal with all this totally out of obligation because I was his wife.

He soon got better, and for the last time I caved in and allowed him to come back home to recover. Secretly, it was not what I wanted. But then he asked me for another chance and stated that being near death had changed him. I still did not trust him, and I waited for the ball to drop. Then we received news that his mother passed away. I began to feel sorry for him and thought for a moment that maybe these series of events had really changed him. I was like, okay, maybe he is trying to change. I had always had doubts in the back of my mind, and this time I promised myself that if anything else ever happened this was the end of the line. I no longer had the strength to ride.

On October 31; I stayed home sick from work. I had an appointment for my car to have an oil change, and I could not go. I asked him if he would take the car. He convinced me that he could be trusted. I gave him my debit card, but I was not too worried because it had less than 100 dollars in the bank. Soon the clock began to tick, and hours had passed. When he did not answer his phone, I knew that it was a wrap. I acted quickly and changed the pin number on my debit card. My grandson was nine years old at the time, he and I sat on the porch inside the gated community where we lived awaiting his return; I walked to the front of the gate and noticed my car. I walked out of the gate onto the street and saw him. As I got closer, I noticed that he was not alone, a woman was sitting in the car with him smoking crack. I suddenly became the Tasmanian devil. I ran towards the car, he saw me and, in haste, to get away he backed my car into a tree, then took off.

It was over! Finally, I felt no guilt, no shame, and had no regrets. While I wish him no ill will and pray that he recovers one day, I had to regain my life, dignity, and identity. I needed to realize that I did not want to compete with crack cocaine. While I loved him dearly, it was not my fate to live like that. Addiction is real. I wasted many years feeling guilt and shame, and I finally forgave myself. I also understood that some people set out to deceive you; you must really do your digging and find out everything about them. I found out that he had lied to me about a few things. One of the things was that he had never been clean any longer than six months and that the pattern was always the same.

I reinvented myself after this. I found myself afraid and I had negative about relationships. My first marriage was not a good one. But I did the work, and I understood what happened; I was young. But for this second marriage, I was not young; I stopped beating myself up because I could not believe how I allowed this to happen. I acknowledged that it did happen and moved forward. I saw a therapist and worked on myself.

I survived and made it over, and you will too.

BIOGRAPHY: Sheree is a certified Life Coach Specializing in showing women how to use their "Resilience to heal from bad (Narcissistic) relationships that have impacted their self-esteem. She is a Multi-Self Published Author, International Speaker & Master Group Facilitator, and Podcast Host. +Her main goal is to help women move forward while realizing their worth and potential.

+She is the founder of Innovating Life Coaching Solutions, LLC where she offers individual and group coaching programs along with a monthly membership.

+She has helped her clients realize that there is life after a bad relationship, and how to get rid of the hurt, guilt, and shame that comes with unhealthy relationships.

+She has spoken to 1000's both in-person and virtually worldwide and has impacted the lives of many women and children in mind, body, and soul.

Sheree has a true passion for speaking and empowering audiences. She has a love for the stage and when you get a chance to hear her, she will leave you feeling empowered and inspired to move forward.

25

The Courage to Leave Fear Behind!

By: Tiffany D. Bell

It was an early Thursday morning. My husband was sitting on the side of the bed, telling me softly that it was time to wake up. He was already dressed. I had gotten to bed a little later than usual the night before and really wanted to continue to sleep.

"Tiff," he said, "You've got to get going. You are going to be late to work." I slowly came to my senses. I looked up at him as he smiled and bent over to kiss my forehead.

I met Ken after his car flipped while on a road trip to his

hometown near Myrtle Beach, South Carolina. His family had agreed to meet there for Thanksgiving. It was almost love at first sight. We hit it off instantly. Within two weeks, he told me that he knew that he was going to marry me. Five months later, we tied the knot! I packed my things and moved to Mississippi. He was the love of my life.

Even after I had fully awakened, I was incredibly stressed this morning. I felt terribly uneasy. I did not really know why, though. I also did not have time to think much about it. I hurriedly dressed for work. I did not allow myself to acknowledge it. Our regular routine was that Ken would take the kids to school on his way to his job. After getting dressed, I gathered my things and headed out the door. I hesitated for a moment. I thought, "Should I kiss Ken good-bye or just get on the road?" I cannot remember what I decided.

Once I arrived at work, I felt as if I should give Ken a call. "Why?" I wondered. It just did not make sense. I called him a few times. No answer. About 10:00 A.M. I sent him a text that said, "I love you." Still, the feeling would not go away. By 2:00 P.M. that day, I could not take it anymore. I had a powerful urge to be near Ken. It was all that I could think about.

My boss let me leave early. It was nearly 2:30.

I did not know where to head. I just knew that I needed to find him. I drove over a block near the mall and picked up my phone to give him a call again. This time, a woman answered. That had never happened before. I identified myself to her and asked for Ken. She did not answer me. I could hear her say, "Doctor, this is his wife."

Shortly after, the doctor began to speak.

"Ma'am, I am an ER doctor with Biloxi Regional Medical Center. Your husband has had an accident." I immediately asked if he was alright. After three times of asking him, he finally said that my family and I should come to the hospital to say our good-byes.

Never in a million years did I see that coming. Ken was only 34 years old. He was young, vibrant, wise, loving, and kind. He was the kind of guy that people were drawn to. He accepted everyone. Ken believed strongly in community and taking care of the needs of family, friends, and strangers alike. He loved being a father. Ken knew that since age five, that he wanted to be a dad. He also had an excellent relationship with his mom. He cherished her and wanted to take care of her as she entered retirement age. We thought that we would grow old together. We were supposed to be that ninety-year-old couple holding hands on an evening stroll.

When I ended the call with the doctor, I yelled at God. I said, "This is not what you promised. This is not a part of the plan!" My entire future was lost. How was I going to take care of two boys? I lived seven hundred miles away from my family. His family lived even farther away. What was I going to do?

I grew quiet. I sat for several minutes, trying to formulate a plan. I had to tell my kids. How was I going to tell his mom? The doctor wanted me to come and identify his body. I knew that that was not going to happen. If I did not know anything else, I knew that I would preserve my last memories of him. I was going to remember how helpful he was as we worked to get the boys ready for school that morning. I would remember hearing him singing in the shower. What was I supposed to do about his business, his equipment, the rental houses? All of that would need to be taken care of. It was all so much to deal with.

At this point, I began to address the Lord again. I also knew that my attitude needed an adjustment. I remember telling Him that if this were how things would be, He was responsible for making sure that everything the boys and I needed would be taken care of. It was too much for me to handle. I honestly felt that He was obligated to take care of us.

And, of course, He did.

Immediately, people poured in from all around to help us. Ken was well known among his military family and church family. So many blessings came our way, I could hardly keep up. Not a single thing went undone that year. The comfort and love that we were shown made a difference in my heart.

I learned a lot about myself in Ken's death. I realized that I had lived a self-focused life. I loved God, but I cannot say that I really loved my neighbor. Ken tried teaching me small lessons over the years about love... how to communicate it, how to receive it, and how to reciprocate it. It was not until he died that the lessons began to sink in. I began to want to do more with my life and to do more for my community. But I was afraid. I really did not know where to start or really what it meant to be more, do more, or give more. I had spent so many years living to survive. I did not know what it really meant to thrive.

If you consider having a lot of possessions thriving, then yes, we were thriving. We owned several vehicles, houses, and a business. But I did not know the real *Tiffany*. Who was I outside of the kids and Ken? I was a timid girl that was filled with fear and plagued by insecurity. What was I supposed to do to move forward? Could I do something more with my life? And if so, how? Where would I start? Slowly I began to take baby steps toward developing a life that did not revolve solely around me.

I decided that I would intentionally comfort people with the same comfort that I had received after Ken's accident. I also realized that I would need to put fear in its place. It had held me captive for so long. I had lived such a self-focused life because I was fearful of not having enough, not being accepted, and I feared failure.

To reach my goals, I would need to change my mindset. I would need to see myself in the same manner that God saw me. As a man thinketh, so is he! My first step towards success would be to change the way that I thought. My journey to freedom began as I let go of worldly affirmation. Possessions, titles, education, etc., no longer defined me. God began to teach me that as His daughter, I would have everything that I needed. Since He lives inside of me, everything that I need will come.

Seek ye first the kingdom of righteousness, and all these things shall be added unto you. – Matthew 6:33

I had a new understanding of what that scripture meant.

I would no longer need to strive for success or worry about what others thought of me. I am designed according to His divine purpose for my life. I am equipped for every good work. I am a gift to the world. My light shines so that others can see. My affirmation comes from Him. For many years, I lived life as if I oversaw it. My life is now completely His and He directs my path.

My hope is that you will discover your path to courage. Perhaps, it will be in a common everyday circumstance. Or maybe your journey will be more like mine. God can take a tragic moment of life and redesign it so that it makes you strong, brave, and determined to live life to the fullest and for His glory!

It has been fifteen years since Ken's death. A lot has changed. I have learned that my calling in life is to connect people to resources, people to people, and most importantly - people to God. I now use my life to serve others by way of community and church service. I help nonprofits become profitable by developing plans and strategies to impact their local community. I am the founder of NonProfit CEO, the nation's #1 network for NonProfit CEOs to access the resources, tools, and information to elevate their brand, expand their mission while having a greater impact on the communities they serve.

Let God recreate your tragedy into your mission.

BIOGRAPHY: *Leader, Advocate, World-Class Professional, Best-Selling Author, Founder: Nonprofit CEO Network, Co-Director of Success Women's Conference, recently named a Top 10 Conference for Professional Women by Essence Magazine. Her 25 years of Community Outreach and Leadership training have created a formidable blueprint made for transforming young women's lives. Success Women's Conference is held annually, women from all over the nation flood the MS Gulf Coast to be inspired, connected, empowered, and recharged by internationally known speakers and coaches.*

26

Killing Me Softly... Making it Out of a Slow Suicide

Racquel Rochelle

It's nothing more agonizing than secretly dying from the inside... like having a mental or emotionally undiagnosed autoimmune disease... in which something that was created for your benefit turns against you and becomes the culprit of your slow demise.. In this case, the "something" was my mind...My perception...My imagination.. My thoughts.. My words.. My beliefs... What I considered at the time to be the essence of me.. Designed by God to imagine and believe in things that are not as though they were and then subsequently influence the divine inspired cosmos to perfectly align for manifestation when those things are spoken and carried out with devout faith. That same God empowered essence so potent that it can throw Mount Everest in the sea from just a mustard seed portion. That gift...a measure given to all of mankind, but my essence was poisoned. I had belief, very strong belief in fact, but it was belief in my demise. I saw the world, opportunities, and relationships through the lens of inevitable failure. I had grown so accustomed to rejection that I subconsciously rejected everything that I thought would potentially reject me. I did not give myself a real chance to experience an abundant life of joy, authentic love, and prosperity. This was my undetected condition for a number of years.. How many years I cannot say exactly because I was ignorantly on destructive auto-pilot. But while I may not know the full duration of its existence, I am aware that there was a beginning. I did not exit my mother's womb with a death wish but along the way a wish morphed itself into a strongly satisfying suggestion. I did not consciously want to die but my thoughts and mannerisms hinted that I was eager to transition from this life to the next because I was done living here... I was done failing here.. I wanted so much to feel victorious and my perception was that my reality on this side of heaven did not contain any victories for me.. Only betrayals.. Let downs.. Disappointment.. Rejection... and abandonment. They say the strong survive and according to my criteria, I did not fit the qualifications to enjoy an existence amongst them. So I cut off every ounce of potential enjoyment at its head and like clock-work engaged in things that would bring me heartache and despair. Not knowing what to do with myself if I didn't have a wound to lick, I had gained an obsession with taking metaphorical beatings but again I ask.. where did it begin?

Implantation

I wonder if it's possible to have multiple points of entry...There is a vast collection of events that fed this ever flowing fountain of self-rejection. But as I reflect, I think the genesis of my self-rejection began when I was four or five years old with the dawn of my intimacy with molestation. You may be taken aback by my choice of words... coupling a beautiful word with one that is monstrous.. But this conundrum accurately depicts my experience.. Yes I was violated in every sense of the word, but perversely I liked it.... That's right... I liked it. In my short time of living, I had grown accustomed to being invisible. To me, everyone around me inherently drew love and care from the people assigned to them. Others had "it" factors that effortlessly attracted some form of positive attention be it their appearances, status, or personalities, but then there was just me. Ordinary me... a deeply melanated little brown girl with an overworked emotionally distant mother and absent father. A child who felt like a burden of inconvenience wrapped in the often repulsed darkest shades of melanin. The one who placed a lot of effort into failed attempts of being seen and accepted. I did not want popularity... I just simply desired to be adored. Unfortunately, adoration seemed to repel me, never wanting to be in my company. Yet in these moments of being desecrated and deflowered, I felt somewhat adored... wanted... seen. And in seeing myself, I was repulsed. How could I enjoy something so foul? I had an idea that this act may be wrong but it didn't feel that way. Being a science major, my adult mind now understands the biology of what was happening but being ignorant of this knowledge as a child, I disgusted myself. I was grotesque. In my little mind, something had to be wrong with me. Not my skin nor my hair nor my mind nor my personality but me... the core of me was wrong. This is when I entered into a covenant with shame. This was the seed.

Cultivation

Shame and a deformed comfort drove me to endure and conceal this defiling pleasure as it continued on for the next few years. That first encounter with perversion was the seed of self-rejection. However, the events in my life following provided the environment and nourishment conducive for the seed to take root and bear the fruit of self hatred in the form of self sabotage. It appeared as though I had an internal magnet to rejection, mistreatment, and abandonment. In hindsight considering Proverbs 23:7 says that you are what you think, that may have been the case. The seed may have been the magnet. My experiences were decorated with a diversity of rejection. Discussing them all may require a stand alone book, which isn't sounding like a terrible idea at the moment. But I digress, I will only share a few of the pivotal moments in our time together now. Also at five, I was involved in a car accident in which I was stuck in the car between the dashboard and brake pedal and had to be pried out of the car by the fire department. Upon my rescue, I looked to my mother for comfort even if just in the form of a hug... but the hug never came. Rejection confirmed. When the news of the molestation came forth when I was 9, I expected for my absent father to become so furious that he would finally show up and rescue me... but he stayed put nuzzled comfortably in his absence. Rejection confirmed. When my sisters and I would be looked after by one of my sisters' grandmother, she would not allow me to sit on her furniture when we would watch tv together. My place was on the cold North Gulfport project tiled floor right underneath her feet, forced to inhale the smothering exhaled smoke of her Marlboros, not allowed to go to bed until she was ready for me to. She did not like me and it showed. Instead she tolerated me. Rejection confirmed. (In hindsight, I learned that at the time she thought I was the only one out of my sisters who was not her blood relative...yet still rejection confirmed) In middle school for Valentine's Day, my friends at the time, who all happened to have fairer skin, received an abundance of sweetheart gifts but I was not desired to be anyone's sweetheart. The only gift I was ever offered was a rejected gift from one of my fair skinned friends. A young man wanted to give the gift to her, she said no due to having her hands full already, and so he turned to me and said, "Well here, you can have it." That same twisted "something" in me that caused me to accept molestation rose again and wanted to take the gift and pretend that I was desired seeing that it's the closest I had ever gotten. Rejection confirmed. My first boyfriend pursued me because he was rejected by the girl he was in love with and I knew that at any moment if she wanted him back, she could have him. But that twisted "something" wanted his rebound desire for me even though it came along with unfaithfulness on his part. To add insult to injury, at 17, I gave him what was left of my "virginity." and when he finished (rather quickly), he unsatisfyingly accused me of not being a virgin and left. I mean seeing that I was raped, I guess he was right but... Single..double...triple rejection confirmed. I could give countless more accounts but these are enough to drive the point. Within each of these encounters lies an underlying theme, I was rejected just for existing. I did not bring attention to myself or solicit mistreatment in any way. There was nothing I could pinpoint as the provoker other than being the essence of me. Each occurrence posed as another cement block that developed into this strong core belief..

"I am an inconvenient and undesired afterthought undeserving of any authentic personalized joy or adoration. I am here only to brutally serve at the pleasure of others including God himself."

That truth aligned with my experiences... it made sense. Therefore, it's what I lived by.

Harvest of Self-Sabotage

I didn't realize it at the time but I had developed an attraction to destruction and hardships. It was my comfort zone...it was what I knew... it's what I was accustomed to responding to... Anything healthy was rather foreign to me and I wouldn't know how to handle it. Recently, I was told that in our minds we subconsciously have oversized highlighters and erasers that serve to validate our core beliefs. We overlook, downplay, and ignore experiences and truths that contradict the belief; yet, we magnify and meditate on those encounters that confirm them. I would find myself captivated by degrading situations and I would subconsciously ruin opportunities and experiences that could have turned out well for me. This cancerous way of thinking infiltrated my relationships, career opportunities, and my spiritual journey. I'm sure that I may have had some people enter into my life who saw my value and wanted to love me but I couldn't see them. I had a sickening loyalty to people and habits that tore me down. In high school I was given an opportunity to go overseas and serve as an ambassador of an honors program, whose name I unsurprisingly do not remember. I did not apply. Self sabotage. After graduating high school early, I moved in with my dad in Atlanta to take a shot at becoming an actress, writer, and singer. XXI Century Entertainment took an interest in me but my mother shut down the opportunity. Ms. Daisy Ramos gave me her card and told me to contact her when I got of age, which was only a few months away. Yet, she had never heard from me again... nor did acting... nor singing... nor writing until years to come... Self sabotage. In college, I befriended a group of girls who genuinely cared about me but I would always say to them that, "I don't do females." (hard eye roll) Truthfully I wanted nothing more than to develop a genuine sisterhood with them but here I was rejecting them as a defense mechanism against the rejection I felt would come inevitably from them in due time. Self sabotage. On the flip side, I kept desiring friendships with people who wanted nothing to do with me unless I had something to offer them. Once the benefit was up, they left with it, often ghosting me... and I followed trying to figure out something else I could give of myself to get them to come back... Self sabotage. In terms of romantic relationships, I kept finding myself involved with men who were emotionally unavailable, cheated on me regularly, physically abused me, stole from me, and/or made me feel as though I had to continuously earn their affection. I was the one trying to convince various men that I was worthy of being claimed publicly yet failed. I had a few situationships that involved me giving men money or giving my body to men despite not wanting to because what they wanted mattered most. My desires and needs were a non factor and unidentified because they were a nonfactor to me. I accepted every form of physical abuse, infidelity, sexual abuse, pressure of being a secret, ghosting, manipulation, and gaslighting with self-hating open arms... Self sabotage. At some point I sabotaged myself right into paralysis. I could no longer hope...dream... aspire to be anything great or have anything of value to call my own. I isolated myself, kept my head down, became mute when I entered rooms, and tried to be as invisible as possible. I had no idea who I was anymore if I ever did know. I couldn't tell you what I wanted, what I was gifted in, what I deserved, or what I was called to do. I had no understanding of why I was even created other than for reckless use. I was mentally invalid... a zombie for the lack of a better word. Not physically carrying out suicide attempts but killing every imaginative thought or dream of a better life and speaking daily doses of word curses over myself waiting for the day that I could transition out of this place.

Killing Weeds at the Root

It was here that I was waking up angry with so much attitude. WHY.. AM... I ..STILL.. HERE... This question haunted my soul and seemed to terrorize me because I could never grasp for the answer. With everything else rejecting me including myself, why isn't the breath of life? It continued to haunt me and taunt me and provoke me and haunt me again until the day....it healed me. So far your journey with me has been dismal. And while I am not super proud of the events or encourage others to mimic my path, its damning existence beautifully contrasts and displays the love of God. See the thing about our creator is He creates with intention. Life is never given coincidentally. Every breath is purposefully measured even if the purpose is unknown by the benefactor at the time... and that was me. Comparably to the fountain of rejection, this fountain of healing also has a vast collection of events that feed into it even still today as healing is a journey with multiple levels of attainment. The most impressive event was the discovery of my birth certificate. While helping my mother look through her chest of papers for something, I stumbled across it. And in looking it over, I saw the most numbing information. I was born on 5/13 at 5:13AM... I just sat breathlessly holding that paper for what seemed like a lifetime. In that moment, I could not say anything but the Holy Spirit said everything...

"You are not a mistake."

Hearing this truth sent me on a worldwind.. My date and time of entry could have been a coincidence but that did not settle in my soul as so. It's as if God knew, of course he did, that I would enter into this seemingly never ending vortex of worthlessness and so He orchestrated my arrival in a way to forever contradict that lie. My birth date and time can never be altered or taken from me. It's something of value that's mine... and it was given to me by God...

"I matter to the God of this universe... could I be wrong about how He thinks of me?"

Questions overtook me like an ambitious lifegiving flood. So wait...if I'm not a mistake.. that means there's a plan for me? You wanted me here for a reason? But wait...if your Word says that your plans are not to harm me.. how does my lifetime of rejection and abuse fit into that...and again why am I still here... A short time after, my grandmother passed in a way that invoked even more questions... and it seemed no one had answers but God... I had to face this God whom I had so many wrong perceptions about. And out of all the burning questions in my soul, the main one I needed answered was, "Why am I still here?" So, in my intellectual fashion I dedicated myself to learning what I could about who God was..is... I mean it made sense that if I want to know the truth about a creation, I need to know and understand the creator. But in

God's divine fashion the more I sought after the truth of who He is, he revealed truths of who I am. I had been living out a satanically and cleverly crafted lie. It was impossible to see God or myself accurately through the scaled lens of rejection and deception on my eyes. The seed implanted in my young adolescent mind was intentionally placed and cultivated by a vile being opposite yet pathetically unequal to the God of love who created me. While the seed of rejection brought forth an abundance of destructive fruit, it's more efficient to kill the root than to battle with each individual fruit. The poison implanted in the essence of me had to be extracted.

Through a myriad of journaling, sound teaching, books, testimonials, therapy sessions, biblically sound meditations and affirmations, and change of environment (referencing my tribe), one by one every wrong core thought was challenged and corrected (or is still being corrected...remember it's a journey). As my thoughts of myself changed, those subconscious highlighters and erasers changed as well. I began to see the gifts in me. I saw the impact I made on others. When you see yourself correctly, your expectations and standards for yourself change. When opportunities presented themselves, such as participating in anthologies, I did them...afraid yes..but I did them. And with each opportunity comes more liberation.

For those of you who may have destructive or debilitating thoughts of yourself, a practical exercise is to set a series of quiet times and write out all of the thoughts you have about yourself, even the embarrassing ones. Then look for evidence in your life that contradicts those thoughts and write them down. Are you really a failure? Is there really not any evidence that says you're not? Then next to the lie write out the biblically supported truth and revisit them often. You would be amazed at how much you've allowed to deceive you. Go into these times with God and be honest with him and yourself about how you are feeling. Your anger, grief, and confusion do not offend him. Do not be discouraged if you're doing well for a few days or weeks but then are triggered to believe a lie about yourself again. Allow yourself to be human but remember that you are a human designed for and deeply loved by God.

We're not dying a slow death on our way to heaven. I'm here with you sis. Let's go.

27

Against All Odds, Almighty
God Protected Me!

Coach Tina Ramsay

**Every adversity, every failure, every heartache carries with it the
seed of an equal or greater benefit. -- Napoleon Hill**

Who am I? I grew up in a small town in South Carolina, I am the
only child of two of the most fun loving, and supportive parents on the
planet. They have always supported me. I am extremely close to both of
my parents, and I love them so much. They gave me Life and God used
them to save my life multiple times. They taught me, most importantly,

about the Almighty God and how to build my own personal relation-ship with him. They taught me about loyalty, friendship, love, and that your word is your bond.

Who I am Today is because of Almighty God following the guidance of God's Word the Bible and the fact that He Blessed me with the most loving and nurturing parents ever. I thank God for always Protecting me from Harm and Danger, allowing me to help others.

Please allow me to share a Piece of my Life with you. ALL of my Businesses were Formed through my own personal struggle. Those struggles lead me to finding the solution to help myself, then that solution helped to position me to help others because God is navigating and blessing the way. We are literally reaching Goals and unfolding our dreams together. One day at a time! Reading this you may be saying... this girl had it easy with a silver spoon in her mouth. She could not possibly understand the challenges I face. Well, I beg to differ. My life may seem to be easy, but it is not. In fact, on multiple occasions, I wanted to give up. But why did I keep going? Read the rest of my story to find out WHY!

Against All Odds, Almighty God Protected me!

My Dad and Mom always let me know that my very life is a blessing because according to the Doctors I was not supposed to be here. When my Mom went into labor 40 years ago with me the experience was so traumatic that the Doctor came out of the emergency room and asked my Dad to pick which person that he wanted to survive, my Mom or me. The Doctor said that there was no way that the both of us could possible live. One of us would die. But my dad prayed for my mom and I to be spared, and we were. God had a plan and mapped my life out for me before I even understood what my purpose was. God was and still is patient with me, understanding all of my strengths and my weakness. For that I am truly grateful and in awe of him.

Fast forward to when I was only 6 years old. My mother and I was at a Convention, and I almost fell from a 3 story building, but Almighty God and his angel protected me. I was a child that love to run. So, I remember it like it was yesterday the panic in my mother's voice as she yelled out to me, "TINA STOP!" So, I did. When I turned around, all I saw was the ground below and the enormous whole that was missing from the upstairs breeze way. I rocked from side to slide as my mom cried and was praying to God to keep me save. You see, my mom was about 15 feet away from me at the time there is NO WAY THAT I SHOULD HAVE SURVIVED THIS. I was on the edge of the hole, and I know that God and the angels held me there long enough for my Mom to grab me to safety. My Mom always reminds how GOD protected me that day.

On two separate occasions and both involved me almost being abducted. Let us start from the first time my life changed. I was 3 years old at the grocery store with one of my relatives and I have always been very friendly and curious. I walked away from her as she was shopping and then a women grabbed my hand and quietly walked me out of the store. I was only three and we lived in a small town. The lady was around the corner with me when my relative yelled in the street that lady is taking my baby. At once the women let me go and my life was spared.

Next, at 9 years old, my family and I was out of town and once again I loved to play. My favorite game was hide and seek. I was the best at hiding in the family because I was so small, I could literally fit in the smallest places. I loved to play and explore. So, on this day we were at another grocery store, and I was supposed to stay in the car, but I got out and I did not tell my mom. We were in a big city, and I was excited to see all of the big buildings, cars, and multicultural people. I remember feeling like I was alone, so I was drawn to go to the store door and what did I see? I saw our family vehicle driving on the highway without me. Since I loved to hid in our huge van all of our family thought that I was just hiding again. My heart sunk as I saw them go on the interstate without me. At that moment, a couple walked up to me and asked me was I lost. But it was something about them that I knew was not right. My parents taught me not to lie, but I felt that I had to because at this point, they were trying to get me out of the store.

Then, I remember the story in the bible about Abraham and Sarah. In Genesis 20:1-6 in the Bible states how Abraham lied and told

Abimelech that Sarah was his sister. Why? Because Abraham thought if he told him the truth that he would kill him, and God promise to him would not be fulfilled about him being a mighty nation and share the mother of the nations. Remembering that those scriptures allowed me to muster up boldness. So, I prayed to God to forgive me and I said that couple that my aunt is the manager of this store and I am with her. They said to me NO your family left in the car and I saw them. You are coming with us.

At that exact moment, the manager walked up to me and said this is my niece. Then she grabbed my hand and instructed me to go in her office until my mom comes pick you up after she gets off of work. Once I got in the office with her, I told her that those two people are not my family they were trying to take me. She said that she felt that something was strange about them. God used that manger to keep me safe. Again, GOD saved me from harm, and I am so grateful.

Growing up I always wondered why God had such an interest in me, my life, and do I deserve his favor. As an adult I almost died, I literally saw the light and heard the monitor flatline, but the plea of my mother's tears, voice, and praying to Almighty God pushed me through to live. Through all of this prayer and God helped me to get through and survive some of the most painful moments in my life. For a long time, I lived in fear, stopped traveling, and never trusted anyone. But, by totally surrendering to his love and being obedient to him has allowed me to tap into what love truly is and what it's not.

I said all of this to make it clear that Almighty God (Jehovah) not only protected me within his loving mighty arms from the beginning, but he has continued to do. He has never left my side to this day. He Protected me and have me here for a purpose. I am on an assignment that he designed for only me. Although for a long time I ran away from it and him in some ways because it scared me on how much he is using me to fulfill his purpose. At moments, I still say why? But God is like WHY NOT YOU MY DAUGHTER! So, the both of us are on this path walking together along with 2 beautiful children, that inspire me every day to push myself so that their future with God's Help will be secured.

My family is the core of who I am and what I will continue to become with God's help. I have had so many adversities, challenges, struggles, and pain that at times I questioned God as to why this is happening to me. I do my best to treat others as I want to be treated like Matthew 7:12 says. I only operate to do all the things to build up my faith.

Now, I understand. Why? because God knew that he was going to use me as a vessel to motivate and inspire the world. For me to do that effectively I had to experience it first so, that I could know how it feel. This enables me to be of better servant leader to the people that I am here to service from all over the world. When I speak, I speak from the heart and from the experiences that I had, and not just from a book.

Although, I am a VCM & Mindset Development Coach for Business and Life. I still weight heavily on my experience because your story matters and your story are what changes the world. I realize now that my story, struggle, and challenges happened to me, but it is not for me. My story is for the people who I am here to help. Now, I understand why I have a child with multiple learning differences which includes autism. Now, I understand. Why? I had to Homeschool my children. Way before the pandemic was thought of. Why? I had to go through Financial Struggle and pretty much loss it all. Now, I understand. Why? I had to suffer with my health for 25 years. Now, I understand. Why? I had a stroke at 25 years old, that left me partially paralyze. Now, I understand. Why? I had to endure having amnesia., losing a whole year of memories including forgetting that I was at that time a 1st time mom with a 6-month-old baby. Now, I understand. Why? I suffered in silence with menstrual health problems for 25 years. Why? I experience the feeling of being on the edge of losing my life so many times. Now, I understand. Why? I miscarried my first time getting pregnant. Now, I understand. Now, I understand. Why? I completely lost who I was through years of battling with chronic depression.

My WHY is because Almighty God knew that he could use me to tell my story to help others see themselves through the lenses of my life, move them to action, how I made it over to draw close to him. My Self Now, I understand. Why? Doubt struggled and feelings unworthiness overtook me. Although, my parents, husband, and children showered me with Love and admiration, I was still loss for a very long time. But one day it all clicks for me and my life started to reveal my purpose one layer at a time. Within those layers it slowly started to change me into the woman that you see today.

My Pain, My Purpose, My Passion, and Birth began on April 7th, 2019, Layer one of My life started to change and reveal itself. How? My husband and I were introduced to the most amazing product that changed my life. This product ended my 25 years battle of suffering in silence with the worst cycle ever. No matter what I did I could not find relief. Even with my wealth of knowledge within the natural wellness industry I could not solve this problem. I felt like a fraud. Although with God's help my other health problems was solved but for the life of me I could not fix this, So as I spoke all over about Health and wellness, I hid this secret of how I suffered in silence with my menstrual cycle, but who could I talk to about this sensitive topic and will my suffering ever end? One day I learn about how pads are made, the toxins, and chemical in them and how it could be the problem as to why I was so sick. Well, I decided to give it a try.

Let me tell you this...These All-Natural Sanitary Napkins (Pads) changed my life. NO Cramps, my cycle shortened and now I can live my life even on my cycle. After my amazing experience and my daughters, I started educating Women and Young Girl about this all over at events, camp, school, and more. I am one of this Companies Top Ambassadors. I let them know that Period Pain is now optional. I am Community Partners with the Girls Scouts of America, and I am determined to educate and break the silence on Female Menstrual suffering. Through my Pain and finding my solution it led to me starting my first business HealTheHoneypot.com which is a Google Blue 5 Star rated verified business Helping females all over the world Heal the Mind, Heal The Body, and Heal The Honeypot all naturally.

We are a Natural Female Wellness Business that is known for our Community Educational Work, Classes, Products, and Services. We even make it easy for you to purchase our Natural Wellness products with or monthly subscription that we mail to your home. We are your Wellness Hub for Natural Menstrual Pads, Classes, Essential Oils, Soaps, deodorant, and more. I now understand why I had to suffer in silence for 25 years with my own Menstrual issues. Now, that I have solved my problem and I know longer suffer, I can help other Females and young girls everywhere.

I am so happy that my business Heal TheHoneypot.com is Community Partners with Girl Scouts of Americas on the initiative. I am their female wellness & menstrual health instructor in South Carolina. My personal pain birth into, my purpose, and that turned into my passion and now I share this with world. When the World Changed, My Journey Changed, Not My Heart When the Pandemic hit my life fall apart. No longer could I go to Speak at Events in person, go to school, and organizations to educate and provide my products to the females.

My husband lost both of his jobs. The pandemic even slowed down and then completely stopped my Community Volunteer work. This stopped my ability to get contributions to help females in need. Which broke my heart. To be honest, we are still having a hard time. We were only able to help 100 veterans and girls this year. Usually during this time of the year, we have already helped thousands of females. So here I was at a crossroad about to give up. I had to make a decision close shop or go digital.

So, I Pivoted and started over going 100% digital online. This is a new beginning. It was not easy; my business was hit hard. I lost a lot of money, and like I mentioned before my husband lost both of his Jobs. We were destitute. Both of our vehicles broke down 2 weeks apart and there where so many other problems I am not even going to write them all.

I was God here we go again, why me?

All I wanted to do is still help females #HealTheHoneypot and take care of my family, but how? Then guest what happened? A Major Social Media influencer did a video about my business Heal the Honeypot and it went viral over 66,000 views in less than a day. There were thousands of people who wanted my product and said that they will buy it. I was so happy and thanking God for this blessing. But guess what happened all of those thousands of people ordered from another company thinking that it was my business, but it wasn't. I lost thousands and thousands of dollars in sales. I was broke, devastated and felt like a loser. I invested over 5 figures in my business, and it was not growing because of the Pandemic, and I had nowhere to turn. But I turned to my almighty Protector God because I knew that he was not finish with me yet. Usually, when I start going through so many problems, I am about to reach another breakthrough. I felt a shift and knew that something was going to happen but what I had no idea.

Last year, I went viral as an international speaker because of my participation in the Queen Xperience Tour. We were on over 200+ outlet and was featured on NBC, ABC, CBS, Fox, Sheen Magazine, Digital Journal and other major platforms that positioned me as an International Speaker. My story impacted so many women that my business and name were written in several articles. That news blast is what laid the foundation for me becoming a #1 Best Selling International Author being featured on a Billboard and one of Oprah Winfrey's Ambassador TV Show. From there I was speaking on so many virtual stages, being interviewed on so many shows, Podcast, Radio, featured in so many magazines, and books that I lost count. This all happened because of Almighty God.

Let Almighty God navigate your live, help others first, and you will be successful. Find you a solid support system of individuals who truly want to see you win. Detach from the ones that drain you, only take from you, and do not build you up. I have learned that at times you have to be still to see what God wants you to do next. In those moments you must close out the noise. I am blessed to have Almighty God, my husband, children, and parents by my side. I am also blessed to have loyal friends and trustworthy business partners. Don't ever stop pushing and dreaming even if no one else sees your vision but you. Know that if you just surrender to the process and work hard, watch and see how it grows. Understand that before you achieve success you are going to be unsuccessful first! That's just part of the birth pains of business. I am no different from you. I just started believing in myself, took action, and got out of my own way with God's help and guidance. **YOU CAN DO THIS TOO! YOU ARE NEVER TO OLD TO REACH YOUR GOALS OR DREAMS! DREAMS DO NOT HAVE A EXPIRATION DATE UNLESS WE GIVE THEM ONE!**

Matthew 6:33 (NIV) Seek first his kingdom and his righteousness, and all these things will be given to you as well.

BIOGRAPHY: *Coach Tina is a Award Winning Thought Leaders, #1 Podcast Specialist, TV Producer, Director, 4X Author, CEO of four 5-Star Rated Google Blue Star Businesses called Epic Business Leaders, CTR Enterprises, HealTheHoneypot.com and The Tina Ramsay Show & Podcast which is an IMDb TV Show & Podcast. She has had the privilege of being featured in multiple books, magazines, and has received multiple honors/ awards such as 2021 Women Who Inspire, 2020 Business Leader for The Pivot, Women of Courage 2020, 2020 Influential Women Who Win, Diamond Ambassador Leader, Community Partners with The Girl Scouts of America, Pitch Perfect Winner, Featured Power Couple for Buttercon Magazine, and 2019 Trailblazer Award.*

28

My Faith is Bigger than
My Fears

By: Coach Sonya

"Only God knows where the story ends for me, but I know where the story begins. It's up to us to choose, whether we win or lose, and I choose to win." —Mary J. Blige

This quote resonates with me for various reasons. Book coach and author, Dan Janal said, "Each of us has an obligation to share our story with the world." Like Mary J. Blige, I know where my story begins. I choose to win despite wonderfully terrible decisions, obstacles, challenges, depression, disappointment, abuse and trauma. You see, terrible events in life provide positive lessons—we may not see these positives at first, but they wait on us with open arms for when we are ready to receive them.

First, I must share a glimpse of my life prior to October 24, 2013, a date that I will never forget. A couple of months before, a devastating myopic event occurred in my life. My close friend was murdered by her boyfriend, my boyfriend's older brother. I was very close to my deceased friend as we had a lot in common. One of the most prevalent things we had in common was having endured domestic violence. Another thing we shared was that we both dated brothers who were narcissistic and physically, emotionally, and verbally abusive.

My girlfriend and her boyfriend were called "Ike and Tina" because they fought in public quite a bit. I remember vividly the last day I saw her. They were fighting again and after the fight and he left their home in an angry, disconcerted state of mind. She told me she was finally leaving him for good, and she needed my help to move to a new city and state. I pleaded with her not to tell anyone and to plan and move, in silence. I saw her on a Wednesday, her body was found the following Friday. She was shot multiple times. After my girlfriend was murdered, I lapsed into a deep incessant state of depression. I lost weight, and I was very unhappy. I cannot forget the image of the police yellow tape around my girlfriend's house. Her boyfriend was subsequently charged with capital murder and received a life sentence in prison.

A few months later after the death of my girlfriend, I existed without living. I pretended I was fine, yet I was a walking, living mess—depressed yet functioning day-to-day. I slept constantly; sleeping was my escape. I did not confide in anyone and pretended to have it all together. I was a doctoral student, I owned a local bar with my boyfriend, and I had a great career as a college instructor at a local community college. I also had a successful career as an online instructor and made over $150k per year. But success means nothing without happiness.

The abuse I experienced with my ex-boyfriend was behind closed doors. I did not tell anyone. Often, we love who we thought they were or will be —not the person they truly are. If you are with someone who tells you how to navigate your world, this is not normal. Whew, Chile— this man sold me a wet dream, which quickly turned into a dry nightmare. But I bought the costume and played the part. I smiled for the camera, and pretended like everything in my life was okay, as I slowly died inside and silently screamed for help.

On the evening of October 23, as I prepared for work, something felt off. It was a feeling of dread—of "something wicked this way comes." My boyfriend's cousin and his fiancé often carpooled with me due to car issues. I received a call from my boyfriend's cousin that evening, and he said they decided to stay home and would not need a ride the next morning. He and I discussed feeling strange. Then, he shared with me a feeling he had, and this was a huge reason why he decided to stay home. I thought about staying home the next day, but I had various tasks to complete at work.

That night, I could not sleep. I tossed and turned and thought about my deceased close girlfriend. I thought about our talks and our frequent trips out of town. Our trips were our reverie, pleasant escape from our current negative relationships. I also thought about planning a way out of my relationship. How would I plan in silence without anyone knowing? I planned to leave and start over—even if it meant leaving everything behind.

The next morning, it seemed that everything moved in slow motion. I could not sleep and woke up a few hours early. When I left for work, I wept. I wept and felt grief, anger, despair, and unrelenting sadness. Often, we think we grieve about one thing when it may be a conglomeration of elements. I was unhappy and knew if I stayed in my current relationship, I might endure a similar fate as my deceased girlfriend.

As I drove to work, I was in deep thought about my life. It was still dark, and up ahead I saw a caravan of tractor trailers at a stop sign. One truck stopped at the stop sign and continued across the road, and the next truck did the same. The last truck did not stop, and the truck driver ran the stop sign. I looked over to the right in a state of horror as I witnessed this eighteen-wheeler heading towards my vehicle. I panicked and tried to turn the car, but the truck driver t-boned my vehicle. I remember sadly thinking, this was how I would die. As my car flipped continuously, I thought about my mother, friends, family, co-workers, and students who I would never see again. Although, I do not remember thinking about my boyfriend at all.

After the third or fourth flip of my vehicle, I lost consciousness and made peace by acknowledging I was dying and called out to God for help. I told him how much I loved him and that I was ready to go. I do not know how much time passed by, but when I gained consciousness, my car was upside down, there was glass and blood everywhere, and I smelled smoke. I screamed from shock, then realized I had to calm my nerves and get the hell out of the wreckage.

Photo credit: Coach Sonya picture from the wreck

Two men ran over to help me, and I told them the seat belt was locked. Eventually, they pulled me from the car, and I could hear an ambulance and police sirens approaching. I do not remember anything after this, but the police officer shared with me months later that I said, "I have an 8:00 class. Can someone call my supervisor because I am going to be late for work?" I was airlifted to the hospital, and although I was in immense pain and had severe Vertigo, I had not one broken bone.

The two men who saved my life by pulling me from my vehicle, No one saw them. The EMT technician who took the picture of my car did not see them either, but their red truck is clearly in the picture. I know they were my guardian angels.

I vaguely remember being at the hospital. I was told that I would experience a lifetime of short-term memory loss, and I would eventually need replacement knee surgery. After my car accident, I experienced panic attacks and anxiety when driving. I started seeing a therapist who also informed me that the accident was not my only trauma—grief, my toxic relationship with my boyfriend, and unresolved childhood trauma, involving abandonment issues based on an absent father, would continue to lead to depression, anxiety, and panic attacks. If I did not deal with my issues, they would continue to deal with me.

Over the years, I stayed silent when difficult times became extremely loud. My car accident was a wake-up call that prompted me to change my life. In the process of changing my life, I had to leave quite a bit behind. I had to resign from my part-time online teaching jobs, and I lost over $100k in income. This income helped me to finance the bar. I also walked away from the bar, left my toxic relationship and did not look back. I refused to mourn a life I never had. I accepted that my life would not be what I thought it would be, and I was okay with this. I had to lose everything to gain everything; I was tired of putting out fires for everyone else while I burned. For me to thrive and live, I had to leave everything behind and start over. When I would think about what I lost, I would immediately think about what I gained —my freedom, my self-respect, my narrative, and my life.

During my recovery, I was worried I would not be able to teach. I was a subject matter expert who would often forget things; I had sticky notes everywhere to help me remember. Also, anyone that is close to me knows that I do not like talking on the phone. The irony is that after my accident, talking on the phone while driving eased my anxiety and panic attacks.

Fast-forward to the present day. I still experience some memory loss and excruciating knee and back pain, and sometimes, I still experience panic attacks and anxiety while driving, yet I am thriving and grateful for life. I am currently in a doctoral program, I have a small business as a career coach, and I am a full-time and part-time online business instructor.

Remember all the online teaching jobs that I lost after my accident? Years later, when the pandemic started in 2020, I was laid off. I lost my full-time teaching job. I thought I lost everything again, but I gained everything back. I received unemployment for two months, and through networking with a few other online instructors—whom I thank from the bottom of my heart—I now have a full-time online teaching position and four part-time teaching positions. One of them is with the school I worked for before my accident. I have learned that networking matters, and never, ever burn bridges. I currently help educators secure remote teaching positions with some of the same networking and career goal techniques I have used.

I have learned that, in life, half the battle is identifying and acknowledging that there is a problem and doing something about it, in lieu of pretending that everything is fine when it is not. We often try so hard to belong where we do not really fit. Do not settle and try to fit into someone else's narrative. Embrace your flaws, your mess, your mistakes, your truth. Accept "the happy" when it shows up. Keep your circle small. What has never wavered is my faith despite my fears. I know that, despite all obstacles, my story continues. **I have greater works to share with the world, and so do you.**

BIOGRAPHY: Co-author Coach Sonya is an online college instructor and career coach and has owned a real estate staging business, Atlanta Staging

Creations, LLC, and a bookstore, Books & Beignets, LLC. Coach Sonya has fourteen years of teaching experience and several years of career coaching experience. Sonya also has ten years of human resource management experience. Sonya is a proud native of Atlanta, Georgia, and spent many childhood summers with her maternal grandparents in Detroit, Michigan. She currently lives in Buford, Georgia.

Before becoming an author, Sonya received her Bachelor of Science in Information Systems from Mercer University and a Master of Science degree in Human Resource Management from Troy University. She is currently in a Doctor of Business Administration program at Capella University.

When she is not writing, coaching, or teaching remotely. Sonya spends most of her downtime (what's that?) reading, walking, practicing yoga, traveling, and spending time with family and friends. Sonya is also an avid sports fan. You can find her cheering on her favorite teams (Atlanta Braves, Hawks, and Falcons) at many different sports events! You can reach Sonya as follows: Email at careercoachsonya@gmail.com LinkedIn at: https://www.linkedin.com/in/careercoachsonya/

CONCLUSION:

This book is Your Gift.

As more grey hairs appear in my head, I am learning how to value all things, like a gift given just because, the warmth of the Sun against my face, fond memories of my deceased Mother Pewee, feet that ache from too much walking (I thank God for feet), and the twenty-eight Brave Women who set aside time while working full-time jobs and managing full-time businesses, or both, to write and share their stories. Many of these women, I did not know before this project. All of these women, I am forever grateful. Each story has helped me. Each story is priceless. This is not your average book; it is what I needed. Right now. And I know that you will find value in the struggles and victories throughout this book. I have. I will.

Enjoy & Learn from this Gift,

Dr. Tonya Blackmon

Who is Dr. Tonya?

Dr. Tonya Blackmon is a mother,Nana, wife, business consultant, entrepreneur, public speaker, and author. She speaks on issues of equal pay, cultural bias, grants/business development, and more. Her speaking and media appearances include her signature Journeys to Millions talk, feature spread in 2 Savage and Success Women magazines on her journey and message of building a financial independent life, and a videos created by www.drtonyab.b on "How to Secure Your Own Bag"—aimed at highlighting how businesses can prepare to win BIG government contracts.

She is a 3X Best-Seller Author (Pray, Slay and Collect, & International Women of Color who Boss Up & Boss Moms). Her Most Recent books are #1 New Release 7 Days Dive into Spiritual Success, Boss Nana-How to Actually Become One, is helping businesspeople GET PAID globally. During Domestic

Violence Month, 28 authors collectively wrote "How I Made it Over" Anthology, a self-care guide.

Book appointment https://bookme.name/TonyaB/lite/chat

HUGE THANKS TO CONTRIBUTING AUTHORS:

Amelia Starr

Aretha Ford-Metts

Barbara Floyd Jones

Darshell Andrews

Dr. Carolyn Stephens

Dr. Dawn Menge

Dr. Lovella Mogere

Dr. Sanja Rickette Stinson

Dr. Stacy L. Henderson

Dr. TeKeisha Wade

Felicia Golden Grimes

Gloria Walton

Jacqueline Lulu Brown

Jeanine Bunzigiye

Karen Van Buren

Lanashane O Robert

Marva Brown-Thomas

Myechia Barnett

Nova Speaks

Pamela J. Edwards

Precious Swain Peaks

Raven J Williams

Sheree Alison Casey

Coach Sonya

Tiffany D. Bell

Tina Ramsay

Racquel Rochelle

29

❦

Need to talk to someone, below you can get Affordable Therapy:

Contact Dr. Carolyn Stephens
www.drcarolyn.live

Dr. Tonya Blackmon is a mother, Nana, wife, business consultant, entrepreneur, public speaker, and author. She speaks on issues of equal pay, cultural bias, grants/business development, and more. Her speaking and media appearances include her signature Journeys to Millions talk, feature spread in 2 Savage and Success Women magazines on her journey and message of building a financial independent life, and videos created by www.drtonyab.b on "How to Secure Your Own Bag"—aimed at highlighting how businesses can prepare to win BIG government contracts.

She is a 3X Best-Seller Author (Pray, Slay and Collect, & International Women of Color who Boss Up & Boss Moms). Her Most Recent books are #1 New Release 7 Days Dive into Spiritual Success, Boss Nana-How to Actually Become One, is helping businesspeople GET PAID globally. During Domestic Violence Month, 28 authors collectively wrote "How I Made it Over" Anthology, a self-care guide.

www.drtonyab.com

www.ingramcontent.com/pod-product-compliance
Lightning Source LLC
Chambersburg PA
CBHW070610120726
47909CB00004B/1155